NIGHT OF NEVER

Girl of Glass, Book Three

MEGAN O'RUSSELL

I0742586

Ink Worlds Press

Visit our website at www.MeganORussell.com

Night of Never

Copyright © 2019, Megan O'Russell

Cover Art by X Potion Designs (https://www.x-potion.net/)

Editing by Christopher Russell

Interior Design by Christopher Russell

Printed in the United States of America

DEDICATION

For my mother

Who never doubted me, even though she thinks vampires are too scary

NIGHT OF NEVER

CHAPTER ONE

"Nola!"

Cold. She knew only cold. Unrelenting, irredeemable cold.

Pain grew deep within the ice.

The cold held no power to hurt her. The pain came from something else.

A ragged, itching ache that blossomed at the center of her stomach, tingling like a thousand bugs burrowing inside of her.

If the bugs were going to eat her away, it would be best if they worked more quickly. If there were nothing left of her, there could be no more cold.

Maybe.

Maybe it will all end.

She formed the words in her mind.

More words existed, fighting through the fierce frost that enveloped her.

"If we don't move now, we'll never make it out."

The words faded from her ears before she could think of their meaning.

"She would never, not in a million years..."

A million years. The cold will keep me for a million years.

The pain in her stomach changed as the insects fought for territory.

Endless nothing would be better than a million frozen years.

"She would understand. You don't have to do this."

Agony seared through her chest and shot through her spine as something wrapped around her. The torment flooded air into her lungs.

My lungs. There's air in my lungs. Pain in my spine.

I'm alive.

Nola fought to speak the words.

I'm alive!

No sound came. The frozen part of her that was her mouth wouldn't move.

"I don't care what you want, I'm staying with her."

The air tasted of blood, rot, fresh earth, and something else. Something with a tinge of chemical. A scent she'd smelled before.

Before the cold took me. Before the knife cut me.

"I'm too damn tired to fight you. You want to follow, follow."

"Then let me carry her."

"You will not touch her again, Domer."

Domer.

The word had meaning that brought pain beyond the burning in her stomach.

She had been a Domer. Lived trapped within glass, safely hiding from the end of the world.

Then she ran away.

Running through the city on her own legs. Legs that now bounced uselessly as the person carrying her ran.

Before the ice had taken her body, she'd broken out of the domes. Saved her friends from being locked in concrete cages.

They'd gone through the abandoned tunnels of Nightland and into the city. They'd almost made it out.

Searching for Emanuel, for wherever the vampires of Night-land had found refuge.

But they didn't make it. Werewolves had attacked.

She'd fought back. But the wolf had won, driving his blade into her stomach.

She gasped at the remembered pain. Arms tightened around her, keeping her safe.

Nola!

The scream had echoed from so far away, but blackness had devoured her before she could see who had screamed her name.

Blackness. Then cold.

Now pain.

Pain radiating from her stomach.

Where he stabbed me. I should have died.

This can't be dying. The pain is getting worse.

A stinging, like fire blazing in her veins, pushed farther from her chest with every breath.

"We need to find a place to rest," a soft female voice spoke.

T. She made it.

Nola wanted to smile, but the notion only spread pain to her face.

"We can keep going a little longer," Raina said, the words close to Nola's ear. "The first bit of sun isn't too bad."

"And if you get sick from it?" Beauford said. "We can't find Nightland without you."

"Too right, so keep up," Raina said.

They made it. They all made it.

Thank you for not leaving me!

"We need to find a safe place for Nola," T said. "She's getting paler. She lost so much blood."

"She'll be fine," Raina said. "The chemicals are changing her. That's never a pretty process."

Chemicals.

Chemicals to change me.

Meaning came as pain bit her frozen fingers.

ReVamp. They gave me ReVamp.

Panic quickened Nola's breaths. Fire surged into her arms. She needed to scream, to move, to do something to break free from the pain.

"We need to stop," a voice spoke from far away, the sound nearly too low for Nola to hear.

"This is as good a place as we're going to find," Beauford said.

"There's a safe place in another mile," Raina said.

"The sun will be too high by then," T said.

"We need to stop for Nola," the far away voice spoke again. "Changing with a wound like that doesn't happen easily."

Changing. I'm changing.

"She can hold on."

A *creaking* echoed in Nola's ears, zapping to the center of her brain, waking up the horrible itching insects that had lain dormant in her head.

"Hold her," Raina said.

Pain shot through every inch of Nola's being as new arms cradled her.

They've made me a vampire. Does it torture all of them this much? Raina, how long until the pain and cold leave me?

Please let me speak.

Her body wouldn't allow her to do anything but breathe.

"Let me—"

"Over your dead body, Domer."

Thumping footsteps carried away.

"You're hurt." The far away voice had come closer. "I'll hold her."

"No," Beauford said.

"I would never hurt her," the voice whispered. "You have to believe that."

"We don't," T said.

Something damp cooled Nola's forehead.

The fire sought the cool, racing up to destroy the comfort, boiling away Nola's thoughts.

"I had to save..."

The words wobbled in and out like lapping waves of sound.

"...didn't need your help."

Flames reached Nola's knees, pushing the hateful cold toward her feet. The ice raged, ferociously fighting back the fire.

Let me scream.

"We don't even know if she wanted this, so you can't say..."

"Upstairs will be the best place..."

"...what she needs anymore."

Embers seared the insides of Nola's ears.

Let me slip away. Let me fall into the black far away from pain.

"I'm not letting her out of my sight. I'll tear down this house if you try and keep me from her."

The pain in Nola's head doubled as she fought her way to the voice.

"If you're dumb enough to think I'm going to let you drag her back—"

"The domes will never take either of us back."

Jeremy.

A swooping ache tore the air from Nola's lungs.

Jeremy here. Jeremy protecting me.

"I'm not going to take her anywhere, but I sure as hell won't leave her," Jeremy said.

Jeremy had been there. Had known the domes betrayed her. Used her to murder hundreds of people.

Then she had taken the others and run. Run through the city. Been stabbed by the knife. Been filled with cold that turned to fire.

"I love her. I'm going to keep her safe."

Traitor.

The urge to hit him, to stop him from speaking, drove past the flames, curling her fingers into a fist.

Pain beyond fire surged through every ounce of Nola's body as a scream tore from her throat and blackness stole her thoughts.

CHAPTER TWO

Heavy weights pressed down upon her, leaving only her face open to the cool air.

The urge to move zinged through her fingers and toes, but the weight brought comfort. And, lying still, nothing hurt.

Voices whispered far away. Sounds of life came from nearby as well. A squeaking floorboard as someone shifted their weight. The soft sound of someone breathing.

Nola lay still, letting her mind arrange everything in an order that made sense. On their way to Nightland, they had been attacked. Someone had given her ReVamp to save her. They were still heading to join the vampires of Nightland, and they had stopped to wait out the daylight. Jeremy was with them.

Nola sucked in a breath as her muscles tensed.

"You're awake," Jeremy said. His voice carried from across the room where the floorboards creaked. "You can lie still for as long as you want. It's going to take your body some time to adjust to the changes. It feels worse before it feels better."

Tears squeezed from the corners of Nola's eyes. The foreign heat of them trickling past her temples gave her the courage to move her lips.

"Worse?" The word crackled in her throat. "Worse than being encased in ice and having your whole body lit on fire."

Heavy bootfalls pounded across the room.

"Don't touch her," T said.

"T." Nola's eyelids scraped open like sandpaper, blurring her vision.

"I'm here, Nola." T knelt by the bed, brushing Nola's hair away from her forehead.

"Are you hurt? Is the baby okay?" Nola blinked, forcing her eyes to focus on T.

The edge of the bed hid T's stomach from view.

"I'm fine." Only half of T's mouth curved as she smiled. Purple bruises covered the left half of her face, swelling her cheek past the point of movement. "The baby will be fine, too."

"Good." Nola sighed.

"Nola." Jeremy stepped toward the side of the bed.

"Stay back." T didn't look away from Nola as she spoke.

Pain shimmered through Jeremy's eyes as he stepped away. "I would never hurt her."

Dried blood speckled his dark blond hair, the shiny pink line of a cut in the final stages of healing marked his jawline. The arm of his black Outer Guard uniform had been torn. The marks of fighting weren't as startling as the worried lines etched between his eyes.

Nola swallowed the instinct to ask if he was okay. "What are you doing here?"

"Protecting you," Jeremy said.

"From what?" Nola asked. "From T? From Raina or Beauford? I trust them. I'll be fine with them."

"I—" Jeremy looked up to the ceiling. "After what I saw last night, I agree. I don't think any of them would hurt you."

"Then go home," Nola said.

Jeremy flinched.

The twinge of regret at her words lasted only a moment.

"I can't go home any more than you can, Nola," Jeremy said. "Even if I made it as far as the glass, they'd never let me in. I betrayed them."

"You should drink." T heaved Nola's backpack onto the bed. Blood stained the material.

"She won't need—" Jeremy began.

"I don't remember asking you anything." T dug a water bottle from the depths of the pack. She pulled back the worn gray blankets that covered Nola.

A dark stain marked the center of Nola's shirt, surrounding the tear in the stomach.

Nola's head spun, her thoughts wrenching her back to the moment the knife had plunged into her flesh.

"Breathe, Nola," Jeremy whispered.

T lifted Nola's head, gently pouring a trickle of water into her mouth. The water tasted of minerals with a hint of chemical, like someone had tried to clean the contaminates from the water by adding other contaminates.

"Thanks, T." Nola pushed herself up onto her elbows. Her muscles shook from the effort.

"Careful." Jeremy reached for her.

"Go home, Jeremy." Nola fell back onto her pillow. "Tell them you were trying to capture me. Tell them you killed me when it didn't work. Your father won't be too angry I'm dead."

"I doubt my father will admit to having a son anymore."

"Why? Because you disappeared with Vampers for a night?" Nola clenched her fists. Her fingers moved without pain, the cut on her palm from two days before had disappeared. "I'm sure you can talk your way out of it."

"I don't think so." Jeremy stepped forward.

"Don't touch her." T sat on the bed, glaring at Jeremy.

"They gave an order over the coms," Jeremy said. "Capture if possible, kill if necessary."

"For who?" Nola's heart raced, faster than a heartbeat should have been able to go.

"For you," Jeremy said, "and the ones you took from the domes."

"They wanted me dead?" Nola could picture it. Jeremy's father, the Captain of the Outer Guard, giving the order to kill her.

Did my mother know? Did she try and stop it?

Nola couldn't answer for sure. Tears coursed down her cheeks.

"I was in a search party in the city when the order came down," Jeremy said. "I couldn't let them hurt you. I knocked out my partner and started looking for you on my own. I found some downed werewolves in the street. Knife wounds in each of them. I knew it had to be Raina, so I started tracking the pack. If I had gotten there a little bit sooner, I might have stopped the wolf from stabbing you." Tears trickled down Jeremy's cheek. "I will never forgive myself for not getting to you faster."

"I'm sorry," Nola said. "You shouldn't have—"

"Shouldn't have what?" Jeremy said. "Shouldn't have come after you? Shouldn't have saved you?"

"Shouldn't have given up your home for nothing," Nola said.

"You aren't nothing, Nola. You're everything."

T held up a hand as Jeremy reached for Nola again.

"And I couldn't go back there anyway." Jeremy didn't lower his hand. "They wanted you dead. My father gave the order for your murder. I could never go back to the domes."

"And it wasn't for nothing." T took Nola's hand. "He—we weren't sure if you wanted the ReVamp. Beauford tried to ask you, but you were already fading. The case was caught in the middle of Raina's fight. Beauford was going to try and get it, give you the injection and screw what you wanted. But..."

"I got there first." Jeremy's hands shook. "There was so much blood. You wouldn't open your eyes. I gave you the shot before Beauford managed to get near Raina's case of ReVamp."

"A shot of what?" Nola pushed herself to sit up, ignoring the swaying of the room. "Jeremy, a shot of what?"

"Graylock," Jeremy said. "I had a triage kit on my belt. You were bleeding out. I didn't know what else to do."

"Graylock?" Nola looked to T. "He gave me Graylock?"

"He betrayed the domes as much as you ever have," T said. "Raina's furious he didn't wait for Beauford to give you the ReVamp."

"Graylock is better." Jeremy dragged his hands over his hair. Flecks of dried blood drifted to the ground. "Nola is healed and can still go out in the sun, eat food, and—"

"And is stuck with dome medicine coursing through her body," T said.

"I saved her life, which is what you were trying to do," Jeremy said.

"No. We're her friends. We were making a decision for her she had been too scared to make for herself. You weren't there when we asked Nola if she'd prefer death over being a vampire." T's cheeks flushed as she spoke. "You betrayed her, chased her through the city, and made the decision to drug her. Maybe you love her and wanted to save her life, maybe you just felt guilty for being such a screw up. Either way, sticking her with that needle is the last decision you'll be making on Nola's behalf."

T and Jeremy glared at each other for a long moment.

"My eyes." Nola took T's hand. "Do my eyes look different?"

"No," Jeremy said.

Ignoring him, T examined Nola's eyes.

"You look just the same." T smiled.

Nola nodded. The room didn't spin this time.

Jeremy opened his mouth to speak.

"Where are we?" Nola asked, looking to the one window in the corner. Boards had been nailed across the broken glass in a haphazard fashion, letting the red light of the setting sun filter through.

"In an old house six miles west of the city limits," Jeremy said.

"Raina wanted to push it farther toward Nightland. Apparently there's a safe house, but we had to get her out of the sun and you someplace to rest." T bit her bottom lip. "It was rough for a while. I think you were in pain."

"I was." Nola squeezed T's hand. "But I'm fine now."

"It shouldn't have hurt." Jeremy shook his head. "An oppressive cold—"

"I had that for sure," Nola said.

"And then some unpleasant tingling while the Graylock got in deep," Jeremy said. "There shouldn't have been pain."

"Says who?" Raina asked, leaning against the doorjamb. "Life is full of pain. Why should a chemically enhanced life be any different?"

"Says me." The ridges of Jeremy's neck bulged. "I was given the shot. It felt like I'd been dunked in ice, but it never hurt."

"Had you been stabbed?" Raina asked.

"No," Jeremy said.

"Well, I think we've found the difference." Raina stepped past Jeremy, her black eyes fixed on Nola. "You going to make it?"

"I think so." Nola straightened her spine. Embers sizzled in her stomach where the slash cut through her shirt. "I may not be able to run too far tonight, but I'm breathing."

"I can carry you again," Raina said. "Just don't get too used to the special treatment."

"I'll carry her," Jeremy said.

"I don't think so, Domer," Raina said.

"I gave up my home to protect her. I love her. I would do anything for her." Jeremy paced the room, his boots thudding on the wooden floor.

"I'm hearing a lot of *I* from you." Raina dumped Nola's backpack out on the foot of the bed. "And I think we need to move forward with what Nola wants and needs. I mean, since she is the one who almost died."

"I—" Nola's heart pounded in her chest, the thump of it so strong it seemed ready to break through her ribs. She took a shuddering breath. Raina smelled of blood. Not of fresh blood, or even like the dried blood on Nola's shirt. Her very essence held the scent of blood. Bile rolled up Nola's throat. "I want to eat, put on a new shirt, and get ready to leave." Nola tossed back the blankets. "The farther we get from the city, the safer we'll be."

"Nola," Jeremy began.

"You can come with us. There's nowhere else for you to go because of me. And I can't believe you'd hurt any of us." Nola stared into Jeremy's eyes. "But you aren't in charge here. You don't make choices for me or for anyone else."

Jeremy nodded.

"And if there's even a hint of you trying to turn us in to the domes or betray any of us in any way, Raina has permission to kill you," Nola finished.

"Yippee," Raina whispered.

"She won't need to," Jeremy said. "But Nola, we have to talk."

"It's almost dark." Nola tossed her legs over the side of the bed. Fire ants gnawed at her knees. "We can talk in Nightland."

"This can't wait." Jeremy pulled a silver syringe from a hard-sided leather case on his belt. Black liquid showed through the glass.

"Graylock." The word tasted foul in Nola's mouth.

"I gave you one shot," Jeremy said. "It was enough to heal you, but the medicine is meant to be given in a series."

"Funny how Graylock is medicine and Vamp is a drug that should be destroyed," Raina said.

"You need to be given another shot tonight and one in two weeks," Jeremy said. "After that, it's just a matter of booster shots when something really horrible happens."

"Like when your chest was ripped open." Nola blinked back tears at the memory of Jeremy lying helpless in a hospital bed. "What happens if I don't take the shot?"

"The work the medicine has started will begin to reverse," Jeremy said. "The wound in your stomach will stay healed, but the rest of it—the changes to your immune system, nervous system, ability to heal—will all disappear."

"And then?" A chill that had nothing to do with Graylock shook Nola's shoulders.

"It'll kill you," Raina said. "Your body won't remember how to function at normal capacity, and you'll just stop."

"Okay then." Nola held out her arm. "Give me the shot."

"And then the next shot in two weeks, then again when you get hurt," Raina said. "You're chemically tied to Jeremy Ridgeway."

"How many shots do you have?" Nola asked.

"Five," Jeremy said. "Each guard is sent into the city with two. I stole two off each of the guards—"

"If you say anything other than who tried to murder Nola," T warned.

"—off the guards who didn't need them anymore," Jeremy finished.

"Then give me three and you keep two." Nola held out her hand.

"The injections have to be done carefully," Jeremy said. "To work best—"

"Then give me one shot now, and I'll hold my other two," Nola said. "I'm sure I can find someone in Nightland to give me a booster in two weeks."

"I would never keep the Graylock from you." Jeremy pulled two more syringes from his pouch. "But they would be safer with me. The case is built to pad them."

"I don't want to be tied to you, Jeremy." Nola took the two black-filled syringes from him. "If your conscience says to kill some people I don't want dead, I don't want to be stuck chasing you because you have a fancy pouch."

"Then take the one you need—"

"I need both." Nola held up her arm for the injection. "If I don't have a full syringe, what am I supposed to give Dr. Wynne to study?"

"Nola, you can't..." Jeremy sagged, his whole frame crumpling. The giant Outer Guard, with shoulders broad enough that once upon a time it seemed like he could fold himself around Nola and keep her safe forever, shrunk to nothing more than a boy filled with horrible sadness. "Take the whole thing then." Jeremy unfastened his belt, sliding the case free. "Give Dr. Wynne as much as you like after you've taken your booster. If he's still half the doctor I remember him being, he should be able to do some good with it."

"Thank you." Nola took the black leather case. Inside, padded ridges separated the vials, keeping the glass from breaking and the precious liquid from being lost. Nola slipped the two extra syringes into the case. "Give me the shot and be done with it."

Jeremy looked to Raina.

She helped T to her feet, and both women moved to the head of the bed.

Nola held up her arm.

"That's not—" Jeremy looked to Raina again.

Raina raised her dark eyebrows.

"That isn't where the shot has to go," Jeremy said.

"Then where?" Sweat beaded at the nape of Nola's neck.

"In your heart." What little color Jeremy had drained from his face. "It would be better if you lay down."

"You're kidding." Nola looked to Raina. "Tell me he's kidding."

"Most vampires don't do it that way since aiming is a bitch and it hurts like hell," Raina said, "but yeah, Domer's right."

"Okay." Nola lay back on the bed, the sheets puffing up dust in protest. "Okay, that's fine. I can do this."

"The ice is going to come back," Jeremy said.

"And the fire?" Nola's voice trembled.

"I don't know." Worry creased Jeremy's brow. "Just breathe and know I won't let anything happen to you."

"And know once the shot is in he doesn't get to touch you again," Raina said.

Nola nodded. Her jaw had locked shut in fear.

Jeremy pressed a button on the side of the syringe. The needle grew, tripling its length.

"Close your eyes," Jeremy whispered.

Nola clenched her eyes shut. Her pulse thumped in her ears. Other sounds cut through the pounding. Footsteps downstairs. Jeremy's ragged breaths. Raina's hard-soled boots stepping closer.

A sting pierced her chest. Ice cold pain flooded her heart, racing out into her veins. A scream tore from her throat as everything went black.

CHAPTER THREE

Arms wrapped around Nola, holding her tightly.

Nola didn't have to open her eyes to know it was Raina's shoulder her head bounced against. The scent of blood both old and new cut into Nola's nose. The soft squeak of leather against leather punctuated Raina's every step. The heartbeat stayed steady beneath Nola's ear, despite the extra effort of carrying a full grown person.

Vampire.

The definition didn't bring fear, but all Nola's instincts told her she was right.

Ice still filled Nola's limbs, warning her with every throb that moving would be agony.

She let her mind explore, moving where her limbs didn't dare.

Behind Raina's left shoulder, that was T. Her feet fell heavily on the crisp ground, and her breathing didn't reach the bottom of her lungs. Behind her walked Beauford, his shoes crashing through the brush on the ground without any hint of grace.

Jeremy moved at the back of the group, his faint steps taking him from side to side. Not staggering. Searching.

A twig snapped up ahead.

Nola tensed. Ice stabbed every piece of her. Tears welled in her eyes as she bit back her scream.

"Give her to me," Jeremy whispered.

"Not a chance." Raina lowered Nola to the ground.

Movement rustled in front of them. Like dry leaves crumpling underfoot.

"There," Nola croaked, the single word tearing at her throat as she pointed toward the sound.

"I'll stay with them," Beauford said.

Nola forced her eyes open at the sound of his knife clearing its sheath.

Raina and Jeremy looped to the sides of the sound, creeping through the trees, which towered in the darkness.

Scars marked the wood. Pockmarks from the acid rain that plagued the city, but this wasn't the forest near the domes. These trees had young branches struggling to survive.

Nola turned her head, ignoring the screams of the cold as she squinted at the trees.

The nobbles on the branches were clear. Tiny protrusions where leaves would soon fight to grow poked through the thin bark.

I can see it.

Night darkened the forest with barely a hint of moonlight to give the world shape, but she could see the tree. Not as though a new light existed, her eyes simply no longer required the assistance.

She locked her gaze farther into the trees where Raina and Jeremy had disappeared.

Trees dotted the hillside, quickly forming a wall of wood Nola couldn't see beyond.

The sounds of movement in the decaying leaves carried from the darkness. Coming from three places. But the size of what moved was impossible to tell.

Gritting her teeth against the inevitable pain, Nola pushed herself to sit up.

She swayed as her brain rejected the agony of her limbs.

"I've got you." T wrapped her arms around Nola.

"Get her up." Beauford held a knife in each hand, his eyes flicking between the trees.

"They're up the rise," Nola said through gritted teeth as T helped her to her feet. Or rather the two ice blocks that had at one point been her feet.

"It shouldn't be taking this long," Beauford said. Bruises marked his face and neck. A chunk of his shaggy hair had been torn out. "Not if it's an animal."

"It's okay. They'll be okay." Nola felt her belt for her knife. The black case had replaced the blade. Someone had changed her shirt, too.

The scrape of bark peeling off a tree cut through the dark overhead.

"Raina!" Nola screamed as black eyes caught the moonlight.

A lopsided mouth twisted into a smile. The expression stayed on the Vamper's face as he flung himself out of the tree at Nola.

Crashing carried from up the hill, but the Vamper landed ten feet in front of her. His eyes flicked from T to Nola as he bared his sharpened teeth.

Beauford leapt forward, a knife in each hand.

The Vamper grabbed the knife from Beauford's left hand. Blood dripped from his fist as the blade sliced his palm, but the Vamper didn't seem to mind as he tossed the weapon into the trees.

Beauford lunged, his remaining knife grazing the Vamper's ribs before the monster punched him in the back, sending him sprawling to the ground.

"Beauford!" T screamed.

The Vamper's eyes fixed on T. He opened his mouth to laugh, baring his fangs.

"No!" Nola dove at the Vamper's knees as he reached toward T's throat.

"Nola!" Jeremy shouted as Nola and the Vamper tumbled to the ground.

The ice in Nola's veins shook as she crumbled into the decaying leaves. Pain blinded her, sending bright spots dancing in front of her eyes.

A thump shook the ground. Then a bellow and a *snap*.

"Nola are you okay?" Jeremy's arms wrapped around her, lifting her to her feet.

"Don't touch her." T's voice shook.

"Shut up." Jeremy brushed the curls from Nola's face.

"Where's Raina?" Nola blinked away the spots. "Is Beauford okay?"

"I'm fine." Pain filled Beauford's voice as he pushed himself to his knees.

"Raina went up and over the hill," Jeremy said. "There was another Vamper heading that way. I was tailing him with her when I heard you shout."

"We have to find her." Nola swayed.

Jeremy wrapped an arm around her waist, holding her upright.

"You need to slow down," Jeremy said. "You've still got Graylock working in your system, and Raina will be just fine."

"If she's not, we all die," Beauford said. "You understand that, right?"

"Why don't you sit?" Jeremy said, his hands moving to take Nola's.

"I'll help her." T took Nola's elbow.

"I'm really fine." Nola's legs gave out halfway to the ground, landing her in the leaves with an undignified *thud*. "Shouldn't I be all strong and agile now that I've had Graylock?"

"Sort of." Jeremy knelt in front of Nola.

"Back off," T said.

"Do you want to explain the effects of Graylock?" Jeremy asked.

T didn't answer.

Beauford moved over to the Vamper, driving a knife into his heart with a sickening *squish*.

"Your vision and your hearing should already be getting better," Jeremy said.

"They are." Nola looked up to the trees. "I can tell it's dark, but I can still see. I heard the Vamper in the trees. I can smell the dirt from the domes on you."

"Good." Jeremy gave a small smile. "It means the Graylock is working."

"Was there a chance it wouldn't?" T asked.

"It's never been used on a female before," Jeremy said. A hint of a blush crawled up his cheeks, peeking through the stubble.

Nola wanted to touch the red. To see if it held heat. To know if his face still felt the same as it had only a few days before when they had been nothing more than a boy and a girl who loved each other.

"Why not?" Beauford asked.

"Breeding," Nola said, sparing Jeremy from explaining as the red swallowed his whole face. "In the domes, women have to be kept away from chemicals to make sure they can bear healthy children. They'd never let a woman take something like Graylock."

"Not even to save them?" T asked.

"They wouldn't be worth keeping in the domes." Nola searched Jeremy's eyes.

"No, they wouldn't. Nola, I'm so—"

"When do I get my super strength?" Nola cut across him.

No pity. Don't let yourself feel pity.

"It all comes in stages." Jeremy's voice returned to normal, all hint of pleading gone. "The first shot fixes what's wrong with you.

The second improves you. The third locks the changes in. The others—"

"Bring you back from the brink of death," Nola said. "I saw, remember?"

"Of course I remember," Jeremy said. "I could have healed without the injections. But it would have taken weeks for me to regain consciousness while my body tried to fix that much damage. Better to get an injection and be able to fight again."

"You mean almost die again," Nola said.

"Sometimes they're the same thing," Jeremy said. "And sometimes you don't care if there's not a difference."

Nola's stomach flipped, twirling itself up to the blissful place where reaching out to hold Jeremy would be the most natural thing in the world.

"When do I get to be strong and fight?" Nola asked.

"Your strength and reflexes should start getting better in the next few days," Jeremy said. "It'll come on slowly, so don't push things too fast. Graylock makes you stronger, but bones can still get broken, so can skin. And you won't be fighting anytime soon."

"Why not?" Nola narrowed her eyes.

"You've never been taught," Jeremy said. "Strength doesn't always help if you don't know what you're doing. I was trained in the skills needed to fight long before I was given Graylock. The medicine just helps me do what I was taught...better." He gave a wary smile.

"Then teach me," Nola said. "If I'm going to survive out here, I need to be able to fight."

"Nola, you shouldn't have to fight," Jeremy said.

"I also shouldn't have been used as a prop to murder people or stabbed in the stomach, but we don't always get to choose how things should be," Nola said. "Jeremy, you owe me this much."

"You're right." Jeremy rubbed his hands over his face. "Once we get where we're going, I'll teach you."

"Or she could learn from a lioness instead of a kitten." Raina sauntered out of the darkness. "Do you want to line up body counts and see who's the more experienced teacher?"

"Was there another vampire?" T asked.

"Yes, there *was*." Raina held up her knife. The blade dripped red. "I think they were a mated pair, two hunting in the wild so close together. I'll bet you all are the best meat they've scented in weeks."

Raina crouched, cleaning her blade on the leaves.

"Do you think there's more of them?" Nola's eyes flicked through the shadows between the trees. The dark shapes held magic in them. Details she had never imagined before. The back of one of the youngest trees had been smoothed by something rubbing across it time and again. Whether a person or animal, she didn't know.

Raina stood, examining her knife before sliding it into the sheath on her belt. "I don't think they had any others in their group. Probably holed up in a little cave, having sex and waiting to kill things. But there could be more. We're still close enough to the city that vampires out here could run in to grab some Vamp and a snack."

Nola shivered at the thought of being a human snack.

"We should keep moving," Raina said. "The sooner we get to Nightland, the better. Can you walk?"

Nola pushed herself to her feet.

Raina growled as Jeremy reached out to steady Nola.

"I'm fine." Nola shifted her weight from one leg to the other. Tendrils of cold wound around her veins, throbbing with every movement. The pain set her teeth on edge but didn't steal her sight. "I can walk, but I might not be the best at running."

"I don't think I can run much more anyway." T took Nola's hand.

"I can carry Nola, and Raina can carry T," Jeremy said.

"I don't want to be carried," Nola snapped. She swallowed the bubble of anger that rose in her chest. "We need to keep moving, and my legs work. Why don't you keep an eye out for anything that wants to kill us?"

Jeremy stared at Nola for a long moment, his eyes drifting from her face to her hands. "Just take it easy. Your body is still changing."

"I'll walk carefully." Nola turned to Raina. "Lead on."

"Right this way, campers," Raina said. "We're starting our stroll through the woods. On the list of sights today: dying trees, a few boulders, and the possibility of meeting some fine folks who want us dead. Keep up. You won't want to miss the fun."

CHAPTER FOUR

How much longer?

The question balanced on the tip of Nola's tongue, but she didn't dare ask. Aside from Jeremy's unavoidable offer to carry her and Raina's inevitable snarky response, no one had spoken in the last few hours. The silence seemed like a truce with the woods. A pact that kept their party safe as the trees thinned out, leaving them in an open field.

Brambles clung to Nola's legs, picking away at the fabric of her pants. She walked with her arms over her head, keeping her bare hands above the reach of the thorns.

The protests of the ice had begun to fade. A frozen stream ran through her veins, but the cold had lost its ability to cut.

High silhouettes blocked the stars as mountains rose up in the distance. Nola had always known there were mountains west of the city, but she'd never seen them before. They'd always been hidden behind crumbling buildings.

Is that where Nightland is waiting? Are Kieran and Dr. Wynne high up in the peaks?

Nola took a few quick steps.

Raina turned before Nola could tap her on the shoulder.

Nola pointed up toward the mountain.

Raina winked and kept walking.

"If we're going that far, we won't make it before sunrise," T whispered in Nola's ear.

Raina shot a scathing look over her shoulder.

"How did they evacuate Nightland out this far?" T asked. "All those people trampling through the woods, and the domes didn't follow them?"

"We didn't have the chance." Jeremy stepped up to Nola's other side. "By the time we managed to get out to look for them and establish they weren't in the city, they must have been miles away."

"And you didn't keep looking?" T asked. "Not that I think the domes have any right to come after Nightland, but it seems weird they didn't."

"It's complicated." Jeremy's jaw tightened, and his eyes locked on the mountain in the distance.

"The domes haven't patrolled beyond the city in twenty years," Nola said. "I doubt they'd know where to start."

"Who knew freedom was so close?" T rubbed her belly.

"Not really freedom for people like you." Raina's words carried over the field. "You would starve and die out here on your own."

"Not necessarily," Jeremy said. "These brambles are growing, other plants could grow, too. Set up a water filtration system. Find a way to protect your plants when the clouds turn acid. Build a place with enough shelter to protect you and you could make it."

"Funny," Raina said. "Nightland figured out the same thing."

"And if they hadn't broken into the domes to rob us and kill our people—"

"Us?" Raina asked. "Don't make me question your allegiance, Domer."

"The domes would have been happy to let Nightland go if they'd gone quietly," Jeremy finished.

"Would they?" Nola looked up to the sky. "Would they have

just let them leave? Not knowing if they were building up power out here? Letting a big group survive outside the control of the domes?"

"Of course," Jeremy said.

Nola rounded on Jeremy. Brambles tore at her skin as she dropped her hands to her sides. "Think about it, Jeremy. Actually think about everything that's happened. They wanted me dead. They blew up a bridge with people on it. Everything that isn't serving the domes is a threat to them. And the survival of the domes is all the Outer Guard and the Council care about!"

A flock of birds burst out of the trees, frightened by Nola's yelling.

"You aren't an Outer Guard anymore, Jeremy Ridgeway," Nola said. "Stop thinking like one."

She turned and shoved her way through the brush toward Raina, who began clapping.

"You know"—Raina started forward—"the first time I saw you, I really wanted to kill you just for a snack. I hate to admit it, but I'm glad you're not dead."

"Thanks." Nola smiled. The cold didn't punish her face.

"Shouldn't be too much longer," Raina said, speaking as loudly as Nola had when she'd frightened the birds. "We all need to stay together. Remember, I'm the only vampire in our little pack, and that means more out here than a shiny Domer coat in the city."

"Raina, is there a reason you're talking so loud?" Chills that had nothing to do with Graylock floated up Nola's neck.

"Because it's better to make noise and let them know we're coming from far away than to sneak up on them and let them act without time to reason," Raina yelled.

"Who's *them*?" Beauford asked.

"Whoever Emanuel's decided is meant to guard the path."

A stand of dead trees grew out of the darkness, swallowing the base of the mountain. There were no new branches sprouting from these trees. Thick trunks with knobby lumps that no longer held the promise of growth blocked their path like ill-formed columns sculpted by a clumsy giant.

"Are we almost there?" Hope filled T's voice.

"Almost to the first place we need to reach," Raina shouted. "Not quite to Utopia."

Raina kicked free from the last of the field of brambles and stomped into the trees.

"She wanted them to see us coming." Jeremy pushed the thorns out of Nola's path with his arm. "I was hoping she had a reason for taking us through such open territory."

Nola hesitated, tempted to fight through the last foot of brambles rather than take Jeremy's help.

"Why does it matter if she wants to cut through a field?" She stepped through the gap.

"Because it's a dumb move." Jeremy held the path open for T and Beauford.

T gave a murmur of thanks. Beauford ignored Jeremy entirely.

"If we were trying to get to a secret location, knowing the Outer Guard might be coming after us, leaving a trail through a field would be just about the worst plan I could imagine." Jeremy jogged a few steps to walk next to Nola. "But if you want to give the people we're heading toward plenty of warning so we don't startle them, and make sure anyone who follows us will be visible to Nightland's guards and not able to sneak up, then letting ourselves get torn to pieces by thorns is a great plan."

"You know," Raina called back from twenty feet ahead, "if you weren't a filthy, murdering Domer, you'd make a great vampire. If you had found your way into Nightland as one of us, Emanuel would have found great uses for you."

"I don't know if I could agree to any use Emanuel would want me for," Jeremy said.

"You'd be surprised what desperation makes possible," Beauford said.

Jeremy opened his mouth to answer, then clamped his jaw shut and shook his head.

"Will we arrive in Nightland tonight?" T asked.

"If we're allowed," Raina said. "But don't get your hopes up for finding baby daddy tonight, little pregnant girl. I think you're in for a few surprises."

"Surprises?" The barren trees kept Nola's voice from carrying.

"I've been alive for quite a while." Raina banged her fist on the trunk of a tree. "I've been a vampire for most of that time. Since before any of you were even thought of at least."

"I didn't know Vamp had been around that long," Nola said.

"It wasn't," Raina said. "Not the way you'd think of it. Not the way it is now. Hundreds of different hack chemists brewing batches with no real knowledge of what the chemicals are meant to do and without the equipment to make untainted Vamp. More than half the people who try to become one of us turn out as zombies these days."

Nola shuddered as visions of men and women with sores on their skin and their minds destroyed sent sour soaring into her throat.

"You're okay, Nola," Jeremy whispered. "That can't happen to you."

"Obviously," Nola said.

"But that's because most people don't have access to ReVamp." Raina ignored them. "See, Nightland has Dr. Wynne, and he makes the good stuff. The kind that makes you all vampy without the *delightful* mental changes Vamp gives you."

"I know about ReVamp," Nola said.

"Of course you do. That's what we gave your beloved Kieran." Raina turned to walk backwards, her black eyes sliding from Jeremy to Nola. "Sorry, was that offensive?"

"Kieran used her and betrayed her," Jeremy spoke in a low voice.

"Seems like a theme," Raina said.

"Stop it," Nola said.

"Do you think the only thing Emanuel had planned was a new form of Vamp to build our ranks?" Raina winked and turned away from them, climbing up the steep hill.

"I know he had more planned than that," Nola said. "Kieran helped him find a way to garden—"

"A garden? How fancy," Raina cooed.

"They had more than that planned," T puffed, one hand on her stomach while Beauford held the other, dragging her uphill.

"Let me help you," Jeremy said.

T ignored him. "Charles told me there were plans. A place where the baby and I could be safe. Where we could live and not have to worry about food or werewolves, or the domes."

"Smart Charles," Raina said. "After all, what's the point in ruling a society of vampires if there's no plan for the future? Nightland isn't a street gang. We are the beginning. We are a better hope for the future than the domes could ever be."

"And what sort of future would that be exactly?" Jeremy asked. "A world ruled by thieves and murderers."

"Yes." Raina clapped her hands and looked to the sky. "That is the question. You've finally gotten to it! If thieves and murderers rule, how is there hope for anything but death?"

"Then the domes would have been right to destroy Nightland," Jeremy said.

"Wrong!" Raina shouted. "The domes are the ones who are the killers. Leaving people to starve in the street. Letting children die when they have the medicine that could save them—"

"There aren't enough resources—"

"And where do they get the resources to run the domes?" Raina asked. "The glass for your walls, the fuel for your trucks?"

"The city," Nola said. "They get everything from the city."

"A new prize pupil," Raina said. "All the things the domes need to create their perfect society come from the city."

"They paid for the glass—"

"Not a fair price," Beauford said. "You could work in a factory every day of your life and still have to choose between food and a safe place to sleep."

"You have some competition, Nola," Raina said. "The big guy is right. Work for the domes and you work for nothing. You work yourself to death without even a proper meal to show for it. And it was no better when they brought outsiders into the domes to work."

"They fed the workers," Jeremy said.

"They kept us locked up," T said. "Nola was the only one who even bothered to tell us what was happening in the city."

"Think about it, Jeremy." Nola tucked her hands behind her back, fighting the old habit of reaching for him. "We lived in the domes, sure we were the answer to saving the world. Never questioning the cost of our own survival. The domes only care about protecting human DNA. They stopped caring about people a long time ago."

"It's not all bad," Jeremy said. "You're making it sound like the domes are filled with serial killers."

"They blew up a bridge with people on it," T said.

"People who were going to attack the domes!" Jeremy said. "There were no non-combatants on the bridge."

"Except for me," Nola said. "I was on that bridge."

"And then they gave the order to kill her." Raina's teeth glinted in the faint moonlight. "And isn't she supposed to be the love of your life? First, you let them use her to slaughter all those wolves."

"I didn't have any say in that," Jeremy said. "Nola, you know I never would have wanted you out there."

"And then the people you still seem to be under the delusion are good ordered her death," Raina said. "Think about it, little boy. Really think. About the unforgivable suffering they turned their backs on. About all the lives they ended. About them letting your girlfriend face a pack of wolves and forcing her to watch them burn. Imagine the reception they would have given the guard who managed to kill her."

"I—"

"Don't talk," Raina said. "Just think. As deeply as that dome-crafted head of yours is capable of. If what they've done doesn't make you sick, then turn around and lead your Guard friends to Nightland. There would be no hope for you outside the glass castle of murderers anyway."

CHAPTER FIVE

"Let me help you." Nola wrapped her arm around T's waist.

"You're still healing." T shook her head.

"I feel all right," Nola said.

I feel better than all right.

The thought held as much terror as relief.

As they tramped up and down through the curves of the mountain, the sky above began to lighten with the rising sun, and the ice melted from Nola's veins. Her legs didn't feel tired, though they'd been climbing for hours. Her breath came easily and evenly, as though she were strolling through the halls of the domes.

Even in the dim light, the edges of the trees held crisp lines in Nola's sight. The faint scent of T's sweat filtered past the stench of decaying undergrowth and tinge of blood wafting from Raina.

I could run up this mountain.

The urge to sprint up the slope tickled Nola's feet, but she wouldn't leave T and Beauford and couldn't risk getting ahead of Raina.

"Raina," Beauford said.

"Yes, big guy?" Raina spoke loudly.

The muscles in Nola's neck tensed at the noise.

"If you're lost, I think it might be time to admit it," Beauford said. "The sun's coming up and we've got to get you to ground."

"Are we lost?" T's voice wavered.

"We're not lost," Raina said.

"We've looped up past this rise twice," Beauford said.

Nola looked to Jeremy. He hadn't spoken in hours, but he nodded at Nola's glance.

"Raina, why are we going in circles?" Nola studied the rocks to their left and the downed trees to the right. She had been so busy wondering at the changes the ice had brought, she hadn't been watching where they were going.

"I'm going in circles because it would be unwise to wait in one place." Raina didn't slow her pace.

"Wait for what?" Nola asked. "You either know the way in or you don't."

"Knowing the way in and being able to make it through alive are two very different things," Raina said. "We have to be welcomed in, and that welcome sure as hell had better be coming soon."

"What if they didn't make it?" T leaned heavily on Nola. "What if something happened and none of the vampires made it out this far?"

"They did," Nola said. "You've got to believe they did."

Tears rolled down T's face.

"That's it." Nola took a deep breath, filling her lungs with the chill morning air. "If someone is out there watching us, waiting to let us in, now would be a really great time!"

The cawing of frightened birds echoed from over the next rise.

"We've come from the domes, and for all we know there are Outer Guard chasing us—"

"Maybe not the best thing to mention," Raina said.

"My name is Magnolia Kent," Nola shouted. "I have Raina with me, and T who is carrying a child of Nightland. I have an Outer Guard who abandoned his post to come with us. If you're fool enough to think Emanuel won't want to see me, then I pity the punishment waiting for you if you leave us out here to die!"

Raina leaned against a tree, her face caught somewhere between amusement and disgust. "You just had to push their hand didn't you?"

"Push whose hand?" Nola asked. "You say this is the entrance to where Nightland is. You're from Nightland, T's got a Nightland baby. Emanuel owes me after the hell he put me through—"

"Does that mean we should leave the other two to die?" A low voice carried from above.

A dark-skinned man holding a long staff stood on a ledge ten feet above them. Bald headed with scars dotting his skin, the man smiled as he looked down at Raina, showing his sharpened fangs. "I thought you were dead."

"Desmond." Raina grinned. "I thought you were smarter than to listen to such nasty rumors."

"Hmm." Desmond's black eyes turned to each of the other four in turn, leaving Nola for last. "Nola Kent, none of us ever imagined we'd see you here."

"I never imagined it either." Nola kept her voice steady.

Now is not the time to fight, Nola.

She forced her hands to unclench.

"But I didn't think the domes would order my execution either," Nola said. "So, I guess it's been a really surprising few days for me."

Desmond laughed, the low sound more like a lion than a man.

"Desmond, you know me," Raina said. "How many years did I fight by your side?"

"Too many to count."

"Then you know I would never betray Emanuel. I've come

home, old friend. Let me in." Raina and Desmond stared at each other for a long moment. "I've got tons of fun stories about being locked in a concrete cage, and I'd hate to die in the sun before I can tell them."

"What do you want me to do with the Domer?" Desmond pointed his staff at Jeremy. "Hang his entrails out for the birds? Bleed him for a snack?"

"No." Nola stepped in front of Jeremy. "He saved my life, and he can't go back to the domes."

"And?" Desmond said.

"And..." Nola glanced behind.

Jeremy stared at her with sadness in his eyes. He didn't open his mouth to defend his own life.

"And he has information for Dr. Wynne," Nola said. "About the drugs they've been giving the Outer Guard. If you leave him out here to die, the information dies with him."

Raina raised an eyebrow at Nola. "See, massively important information."

"Do you trust him, Raina?" Desmond asked.

"I trust my ability to kill him if he steps a toe out of line." Raina shrugged.

"Good enough." Desmond stepped back, disappearing behind the edge of the ledge.

"And in we get." Raina strode over to the slant in the mountainside.

From below, it didn't look like the ledge should be able to hold a person's weight. Covered entirely in moss, it seemed like nothing more than an overgrown lump of foliage.

Raina jumped, grabbing the ledge and pulling herself up in one easy motion. "Domer, give us the baby maker."

Jeremy nodded. T didn't argue as he led her to Raina, or as he took her waist, lifting her high overhead and into Raina's waiting arms.

Beauford walked up to the ledge.

Jeremy held out his hands, offering to lift Beauford.

"Not a chance." Beauford stared at the ledge.

Jeremy shrugged and made a step with his hands.

"Fine." Beauford stepped on Jeremy's palms. Raina grabbed his wrists before he could reach for the moss, lifting him straight up.

Nola laughed as Beauford's feet wiggled in the air before he disappeared.

Jeremy looked to Nola. Her laugh dissolved.

"Are you mute now?" Nola strode over to the ledge.

"I don't know what to say."

The hollow tone of Jeremy's voice slammed into Nola's gut. Like someone had punched her right where the wolf's knife had pierced her flesh.

"Let me help you." Jeremy reached for Nola's waist.

"I can do it myself." Nola looked up to the top of the ledge.

"Thank you," Jeremy whispered. "For vouching for me. For not letting them leave me out here. It's more than I deserve."

"I—" Nola dug her fists into her eyes. "Wanting you to not die and forgiving you are two very different things."

"I know."

"And I don't..." Nola's words faded away as she looked at Jeremy. The lines of worry etched in his face were more than any seventeen-year-old should bear. His shoulders were rounded, like someone had shattered the strong Outer Guard he had been. Dark blond stubble coated his cheeks.

Nola knew what his face would feel like against hers. Where on his shoulder her head fit so perfectly.

"I don't want you dead, Jeremy. I've never wanted anything bad to happen to you. I don't know if I could stand it."

"Nola—"

"So don't pull any asshole guard moves with Emanuel," Nola said. "I know you're strong, but so are they. And he'll do whatever it takes to protect his people. He already murdered people in the domes. I don't think he'll mind killing you."

"Are the two formerly known as lovebirds done?" Raina said. "Some of us would like to get moving."

"Right." Nola didn't look away from Jeremy.

He nodded, offering his hands as a step as he had done for Beauford.

"I want to do it on my own." Nola turned to the ledge.

"Aim a little higher than you think you need to. Try and get your palms on top, not just your fingers on the edge. Use your momentum to push up from there." Jeremy stepped back.

Nola stared up at the moss, feeling foolish.

I'm not strong enough to do this on my own.

"Don't think, just go," Jeremy said.

Nola bent her knees and jumped, sure she would fall flat on her face.

But the strength in her legs carried her up into the air. It wasn't until she neared the ledge that she remembered she was meant to grab hold. Her fingers tangled in the moss at the very edge.

"Yes!" Jeremy said. "That was great, Nola."

The moss she clasped in her fingers shifted, tearing from the stone beneath, as she pulled herself up.

With a *crack*, the moss ripped free. Before she could fall, Jeremy grabbed her feet, lifting her so her torso landed on the rock.

"Graceful." Raina stared down at her, shaking her head.

Nola crawled forward onto the ledge. A gap cut deep in the rock leading to an entrance that had been invisible from the ground below.

"It was my first try." Nola leapt to her feet. Her hands didn't ache from trying to cling to the side of the ledge.

Jeremy jumped up in one smooth movement as Raina had. "She did great." A smile flickered across his face.

Nola searched his eyes for the twinkle that should have been there. The joy of being with her.

"Come on then, super girl." Raina bowed them toward the cave.

Nola walked into the darkness, grateful she couldn't see Jeremy anymore.

"Nola?" T said.

Even in the darkness of the tunnel, Nola could see T's silhouette.

"I'm right here." Nola took T's hand, walking next to her, trailing her free hand along the rock walls.

The path sloped up, leading them deeper into the mountain.

A hint of panic seized the edges of Nola's heart.

You've already died. The middle of a mountain can't hurt you any more than the world already has.

"Are you the only welcoming committee?" Raina asked.

"Don't be offended," Desmond said, his voice rumbling from up ahead in front of the shadow that was Beauford. "We didn't think it was really you. Once I knew it was, too strong a greeting—"

"Seemed likely to get whatever hot headed children Emanuel put this far out on the perimeter killed?" Raina said.

"It's good to see your time with the Domers didn't change you," Desmond said.

"Some things never change, old friend. It would take more than concrete walls and starvation to break me."

Light glimmered in the tunnel up ahead. Nola squinted, trying to decide if the light was electric or only torches like the ones she'd seen in the tunnels of Nightland far beneath the city.

"How is he?" Raina asked.

"Triumphant."

Nola could almost hear the smile in Desmond's voice.

They rounded the corner, and the source of light came into view. Neither of Nola's guesses had been right. A section of the tunnel wall had been cut away, giving a view of the valley beyond.

Far below, at the bottom of the mountain's slope, the limbless trees met the field of brambles. Then the woods with trees fighting to survive where they had met the Vampers hours before.

Beyond the trees, glinting in the light of the rising sun, the city peered up.

"It's still burning." T tightened her grip on Nola's hand.

"It's been burning for a few nights," Desmond said. "We thought the whole place might be done for."

"It almost was." Nola watched the gray smoke twisting into the sky.

"It looks so small from here," Beauford said. "I lived my whole life there, never even crossed the river until the domes came for workers."

"I can't see the domes behind the smoke," T said.

Nola squinted through the gray. A glint touched the hill on the far side of the river, but she couldn't see the sweeping glass domes that had been her home.

"They're still there," Raina said.

"They were built to survive the end of the world," Nola said.

"Like warts from a disease," Raina said. "Awful to get rid of."

"Come on." Desmond moved beyond the light.

The path continued, stretches of darkness broken by swatches of light where windows had been made to view the outside world.

As the sun grew strong, Raina and Desmond hugged the inside edge of the tunnel, carefully keeping out of the light.

"What would happen if you stood in the light?" Nola asked as the bright beams warmed her face.

"Have you ever seen someone with an allergy be stung by a bee?" Raina said. "It's like that, but with a lot of bleeding."

"It won't be like that for you." Jeremy stepped up behind Nola's shoulder, speaking softly though there was no chance of Desmond and Raina not hearing. "You'll always be safe to be in the light. I promise."

Desmond's footfalls slowed. "I'm sure Dr. Wynne will be interested to hear what's left your blood smelling so strange."

"I smell?" Nola sniffed the back of her hand. "What do I smell..."

The question drifted from her mind as the tunnel in front of them widened to an open door leading to a cavern large enough to swallow Bright Dome whole.

CHAPTER SIX

The roof of the cavern towered forty feet overhead. Electric bulbs strung together with thick black wires shed light on every corner. A few tables with chairs and a few dozen cots lined the sides of the great room. Cages filled with weapons from Guard guns to crossbows and swords had been cut into the stone walls. The center of the cavern had been left open. Painted squares marked the floor, boxing in sparring pairs.

All sparring stopped, and sixty vampires stared at them as Desmond led them into the cavern. All had black eyes. All held weapons.

"This is more like it," Raina said.

"Desmond." A woman with platinum blond hair sauntered forward, a sword held in each hand. "Did you make some new friends, or find us a snack?"

Jeremy stepped in front of Nola, his hands raised and ready to defend.

"Friends," Raina said. "I'm surprised they've started letting you touch the pointy objects, Stell. Weren't you just meant to be a pretty face?"

Stell growled.

The other vampires moved in toward their group.

"Raina, you're alive?" asked a man with blood dripping from a cut on his head.

"Yes, I know, quite a miracle." Raina stepped in front of Desmond. "I'm alive, and I've brought some presents for Emanuel. You"—Raina pointed at a reedy-looking boy who didn't appear old enough to have survived being given Vamp—"run ahead to the library. If Emanuel isn't there, find him and bring him to me."

The boy bowed and ran toward the back of the cavern.

"Bring a snack, too!" Raina shouted after the boy.

"Where have you been?" the bleeding man asked.

"Hell," Raina said. "And I'll tell everybody all about it, just as soon as I've told Emanuel. Now, give it up, lover boy." Raina reached for Jeremy's belt.

Hs face flushed bright red, but he didn't fight as she unfastened his belt and took both holstered guns.

"Make a little stash for me." Raina tossed the holstered weapons to the bleeding man.

He bowed and headed for the weapons cages on the side of the room.

The crowd parted as Raina led them forward. Not even Stell stood in her way.

Nola kept her eyes front as they passed through the vampires. All of them held weapons. Any of them could kill her if they wanted to.

Jeremy won't let them. Even without weapons he'll protect me.

She didn't realize she had drifted closer to him until the back of her hand brushed against his.

Don't be stupid, Nola.

She tucked her hands behind her back.

New blood shone red on the floor, spattered across the brownish-black of dried blood from older fights.

"Back to work!"

Nola jumped at the shout. Before they'd made it to the far side of the cavern, the *clang* of steel on steel echoed off the walls.

"What are they training for?" Nola whispered.

"We're not naïve enough to think the domes will leave us alone forever," Raina said. "The domes will try and attack, or the wolves, or a horde of zombies will catch the scent of blood and come looking for a feast. Arriving in Utopia doesn't end the battle. It only gives you more to lose."

A thick metal door set into the stone wall waited open at the edge of the cavern. The metal was four inches thick, and the wall had been carved to receive six heavy bolts to fasten the door in place.

"How long have you been building this?" Beauford asked. "You didn't decide to dig these tunnels right before you attacked the domes, or even in the last year."

Desmond took the lead through the tunnel. Electric lights had been set into the ceiling, bathing the smoothly carved stone walls in an even glow.

"I'm really starting to like you, big guy," Raina said. "Emanuel has been planning for a better world for a very long time."

"Then why is he just now coming here?" Nola said. "He could have left the city ages ago. There would have been no fighting with the domes—"

"And you'd still be safe behind glass?" Raina said.

"It would have been better for everyone." Pain cut through Jeremy's words.

"They didn't move into the domes until the final pane of glass had been sealed in place," Desmond said. "We couldn't move until everything was ready."

"And that took a very long time," Raina said. "I'm so glad I didn't die before I got to see the wonder of the true Nightland."

"Where is everyone else?" T said.

"If you're hoping for a cafeteria, you're out of luck." Raina glanced over her shoulder. "Don't worry, baby machine, I'll put out a call for the sperm donor and see who can find him."

"Thank you." T dragged her fingers through the tangles in her hair.

"How many people live here?" Nola took T's hand.

"I think I missed the census," Raina said.

"Over a thousand, including vampires, non-changed humans, and children," Desmond said.

"There are humans here?" Beauford asked.

They reached a fork in the tunnel. Desmond led them down the right hand side.

"Some," Desmond said.

Lambs living amongst the lions. Normal people sleeping in the safe haven made for those who would use them as a meal.

"Are you keeping them locked up?" Jeremy asked. "Are you keeping the humans caged as food?"

"Yes, little piggy, and you'll be next," Raina said.

"Emanuel wouldn't do that," Nola said. "Vampires in Nightland aren't allowed to drink from unwilling humans. Most live off animal blood. If humans are bleeding to feed vampires, they're making that choice themselves."

"Well done, Nola," Raina said. "Emanuel will be pleased to know all his work on you wasn't wasted."

"Was this work leading up to Emanuel blasting away part of the domes and killing innocent citizens, or was it some other thing?" Jeremy said.

Desmond tightened his grip on his staff.

"Something quite different." Raina laid a hand on Desmond's shoulder. "Emanuel had a strange notion that Nola might be proof there's hope for humanity. One heart that hadn't been so frozen by privilege it could no longer bleed."

"Well, he should congratulate himself then." Tears stung the corners of Nola's eyes. "My heart keeps getting torn apart again and again, and it always bleeds like hell."

T squeezed Nola's hand.

The tunnel branched off three ways. Desmond took a sharp left into a wider tunnel. Wooden doors dotted this corridor, and people moved through the hall.

A man so tall he had to bow his head to walk through the tunnel sniffed the air as he passed, looking from Nola to Jeremy.

A green-eyed woman led four children down the hall, holding a fifth in her arms. She spotted T's belly. "Congratulations," the mother said with a smile.

"Thank you." T watched the children until they were out of sight, trusting Nola to guide her. "Did you see them?" Tears rolled gently down T's face. "They all had color in their cheeks, and so much hair."

"They were beautiful," Nola said.

"They were healthy," Beauford said.

"I wish Catlyn had seen this place," T whispered.

"You made it here," Beauford said. "That would have been enough for her."

"What happened to her?" Jeremy asked.

"Do you actually care?" Beauford said.

"The domes wanted Nola dead, and Catlyn helped keep her alive," Jeremy said. "I absolutely care."

"*All lives have value* would have sounded better, lover boy," Raina said.

A hollow pain swelled at the center of Nola's chest. "We were attacked before we ever got into the city. Catlyn didn't make it."

"I'm so sorry," Jeremy said. "She seemed like a really nice woman."

"She was," T said. "Maybe if the baby's a girl, I can convince Charles to name her after Catlyn."

"Catlyn would like that," Nola said.

Desmond stopped in front of an intricately carved double door.

"Only the best for Emanuel." Raina shoved the doors open.

Four stained glass chandeliers cast colorful light on the room, which was big enough to hold the largest house in the domes. Bookcases lined the walls with paintings and tapestries hanging above. A single door at the far side of the room was the only other exit.

"It's just like Nightland." Nola's throat tightened.

A lifetime ago, she had stood in Emanuel's library, desperate to know if Kieran was alive. She had thought the tunnels of Nightland were destroyed, a casualty of attacking the domes. But Emanuel had remade his sanctuary, preserving his precious proof of what being human used to mean.

A stuffed red armchair, which looked like something out of an old gothic novel, sat in the middle of the room. The seat hadn't been in the library in Nightland. Nola kept her eyes focused on the chair, ignoring the rumble of voices behind the door in the back of the room and Jeremy inching closer to her.

"Raina." Emanuel's voice carried from the door behind them. "I thought I had lost you."

"Not so lucky." Joy filled Raina's voice. "I've come home, Emanuel."

"Thank you for fighting your way back to us. Who have you brought with you?"

There were swirls in the stitching of the chair. A twirling pattern that held no meaning.

"Jeremy's a disgraced Outer Guard who wants to see Dr. Wynne. Beauford was taken to the domes as a worker, so was T— she's carrying a child of Nightland. They helped Nola and me escape."

"Nola." Emanuel stepped in front of Nola, blocking the chair from view.

Curling black hair hung around his shoulders. His eyes were so dark, they moved beyond a given color and into a void of nothing. The natural tanned tone of his skin had been only slightly paled by years away from the sun.

"Nola, you've come back to us." Emanuel reached for her.

"You son of a bitch." Arms locked around Nola before she could launch herself at him. "You made me trust you. You convinced me to help you!"

"You saved an innocent child," Emanuel said.

"And you killed innocent people in the domes. Look at all you built here. Why break in? Just to prove you could? To spit in the face of the domes one more time before you disappeared?" Nola fought against the arms that held her. She would scratch his eyes out, then punch through his chest until she could rip out his heart.

"We needed supplies," Emanuel said.

"You could have asked for them in the trade." Nola's shout echoed off the walls. "Remember that? The time you handed me over to the domes when I wanted to stay with you. Why bother trading? Why bother sending me back if you were just going to break in anyway?"

"There were things we couldn't ask for," Emanuel said. "What we took from the domes will keep the children of Nightland healthy and safe for a hundred years. Is it not worth a few Domer lives to save four generations of children?"

"You sick bastard."

"This is a war, Nola Kent," Emanuel said. "You've known that since the first time you knocked to get into Nightland. It's a war the domes hide from their people, and yet one of their soldiers stands behind you."

Nola glanced down. It was Jeremy who held her in his vise-like arms.

"All I want for my people is to live in peace," Emanuel said. "But one final battle had to be fought. And I did everything I could to minimize loss of life on both sides."

"Tell that to the civilians killed in the domes. And what about the vampire that bit me? Huh? Was he just aching for a snack?"

"They scented blood and a frenzy took over," Emanuel said.

"Not all of my soldiers were as strong as I believed them to be. Bringing the weak ones in was a mistake."

"A mistake that got people killed," Nola said.

"That isn't the first blood on my hands I regret, and I doubt it will be the last." Emanuel examined his impeccably clean palms. "It's the burden of power, and the plague that touches all at the end of the world who refuse to go gently into the dark night."

"You can justify anything, can't you?" Nola said.

"Anything that gives my people a better chance of survival. The domes were wrong to lock themselves away and hoard every resource the rest of us need to survive, but they got one thing right. You can't save everyone. You can't make them all follow you to salvation," Emanuel said. "I gathered those I could, as many as I could, and I found them safety. The few who perished along my path are nothing to the number I have saved."

"Tell that to the families they left behind," Jeremy said.

"I'm still comforting my own who lost loved ones to the domes," Emanuel said. "And now you're here. That either makes you enemies in my halls, or my own family to protect. I will leave that choice to you."

"Are you going to attack the domes again?" Jeremy asked.

"What would I gain tactically from attacking the domes from this distance?" Emanuel sat in his red chair.

"Nothing," Jeremy said. "They would be ready, they would destroy you, and they would follow the stragglers home."

"Then you have your answer." Emanuel spread his hands.

"Nothing about how you have what you need and causing any more bloodshed is a horror you won't risk?" Nola asked.

"That's more true than you know," Emanuel said. "But you won't believe me. Jeremy knows the truth of tactics. That he can believe."

"It would be suicide for them to attack again," Jeremy said.

"Good," Nola said.

"Are you past wanting to attack me?" Emanuel asked.

"No," Nola said. "But it wouldn't be a *tactically sound* decision."

"I think you can let Nola go, Jeremy," Emanuel said. "Learning to live in Nightland won't be an easy transition for either of you, but know you are welcome and will find safety within my home."

"Just like that?" Nola said. "You'll welcome us with open arms?"

"You helped Raina," Emanuel said. "The least I can offer you is a chance at a home."

"What sort of home are you offering?" Jeremy eased his grip on Nola, though he didn't let her go. "A bunker in a mountain, is this really the hope you've been waiting for? How are you going to feed a thousand people? What plants can you grow in the dark to feed the children, and where are you getting blood from?"

"I always suspected the Outer Guard were smarter than their uniforms let on," Raina said.

"I would be happy to give you a tour of our gardens and farm, but it's better to wait for nightfall," Emanuel said. "We have plenty to do in the meantime. Find you a place to rest—"

"And Charles." T stepped forward. "My baby's father is Charles. He fought with you at the domes."

Emanuel's brow wrinkled. "Desmond, find Julian and have him search the records for Charles."

Desmond strode toward the door at the back of the library.

"We'll do what we can to find him," Emanuel said.

"Thank you." T gave a small bow.

The door at the back of the library swung open before Desmond reached for the handle. A boy with dark hair and a pale face stepped into the library.

"We need to get her fed, too," Raina said. "I pushed her hard to get here."

The boy's eyes weren't the green they should have been. Black had swallowed the color.

"Nola."

The boy's voice was the same. She would recognize the way he said her name even after a hundred years.

"Nola, how did you get here?"

The room swayed as he came toward her, worry and joy marking his face in equal measure.

She didn't know how she broke free of Jeremy's arms, didn't feel her feet carry her toward Kieran, couldn't hear the words his mouth formed.

Nola didn't know anything until pain shot through her knuckles as they met his face.

CHAPTER SEVEN

"Nola!" Jeremy's shout echoed off the walls as Nola punched Kieran again.

"You filthy traitor!" The scream tore from Nola's throat as Jeremy's arms locked around her again, lifting her feet from the floor. "You knew them. The people you helped Nightland kill in the domes, you knew them!"

"Nola." Kieran's eyes were wide with shock.

"How could you?" Nola kicked back, catching Jeremy in the knee. "I trusted you. Was everything a lie? Did you ever even give a shit about me?"

"I have always loved you," Kieran said.

Jeremy's grip loosened.

Nola launched away from him, tackling Kieran to the ground with strength she didn't recognize.

"Don't you dare!" She punched him in the chin. "Don't you fucking dare. You led them into our home." She hit him again. "I got bit, Jeremy almost died. So many people did die." She hit him again and again. Hands forced her arms to her sides, lifting her away from Kieran. "No, let me go. You let me go."

Desmond kept her arms pinned.

Kieran stared up at her from the ground. Blood trickled from his nose, and bruises covered his face.

"You were my best friend." Tears coursed down Nola's cheeks. "I loved you. I mourned for you. How could you?"

Kieran sprang to his feet like she hadn't hurt him at all. "We had to go into the domes. There was no other way. I'm sorry."

"*Sorry* doesn't bring people back to life." Nola kicked and squirmed, desperate to break free, to hurt Kieran. To make him feel every ounce of agony he had caused. "You made me believe in you, and then you ruined everything."

"I'm so sorry." Kieran took a step forward, both hands out as though approaching a wounded animal. "I wish there had been another way to get the medicine to save Eden. I wish I had never led you to Nightland and we hadn't needed the supplies from the domes. I wish my dad and I had never gotten kicked out of the domes and you and I were still living there safely, the two of us together, like it was meant to be."

The will to fight left Nola's limbs. Desmond loosened his grip on Nola, setting her back on the floor.

"Nola, I'm sorry," Kieran whispered. "I never, ever wanted to hurt you."

"Well, you did." A sob hitched in Nola's chest. "You broke my heart. I trusted you, and loved you, and..." There were no more words, just tears.

Arms wrapped around Nola. Not holding her back but comforting her. Jeremy held her close to his chest, his scent of fresh earth filling her lungs.

Nola pushed away from him, smacking him hard across the face.

Jeremy blinked wide-eyed at her.

"Don't pretend you didn't hurt me too." Every inch of Nola's body shook as tears streamed freely down her face.

"It's okay, Nola." T took her hand. "You're okay. We'd like to find a place to rest, please."

Nola couldn't see past her tears as T led her out the double door of the library and down the hall.

Emanuel and Raina spoke softly at the front of the group. The sound of Jeremy's boots echoed far behind.

"How?" Nola asked. "How did all of this happen?"

"The end of the world sucks," Beauford said. "Surviving is hard, and it makes people hard. Death is common, pain is normal. When finding a way to live to the end of the day is a battle, it's easy to think of everyone as a casualty of war."

"Big guy is smart." Raina stopped at a wooden door. 113 had been carved at the top. "In you get. I'll bring some food around later." She swung open the door, bowing them in. "Nola, do you still eat?"

"Yes, she eats," Jeremy said.

"Don't speak for me," Nola growled.

T dragged her into the stone room.

"I don't think so, lover boy." Raina blocked Jeremy at the door. "We'll find a different place for you to rest your weary head."

"I—" Jeremy began.

Nola stopped him with a glare.

Jeremy shrugged and stepped back.

"Get some rest." Raina shut the door, leaving Nola with T and Beauford.

Four cots and a table took up most of the room, leaving barely enough space for the three sets of drawers crammed between the beds. None of the furniture matched, and all of it had been patched up in some way.

"They must have scavenged all over the city." T pulled out one of the four chairs and sat, hands draped over her belly.

"How many carved out rooms are there in this place?" Beauford asked. "How long did it take them to dig, and how did the whole thing not collapse?"

"No idea." Nola's voice shook.

"Come sit." T nudged a chair with her toe.

"I don't want to sit." Nola buried her face in her hands. The pain in her knuckles from punching Kieran had already begun to fade.

"Then what do you want to do?" T asked.

"Punch some more people is my guess." Beauford sat on the bed nearest the door.

"That would be nice. Or I could run until my legs fall off. Or grab a pick and smash the walls until this whole place caves in." Nola paced in front of the door.

"You're stronger now, but I think the mountain might still win," T said.

Nola examined the skin on her knuckles. She hadn't even noticed she'd been bleeding, but drying blood coated her hand, surrounding freshly healed skin.

"I hope I'm strong enough that it actually hurt him." A tremble of shock stung Nola's heart at her own words. She sank into a chair.

"I didn't know you'd really been in love with him," T said. "Kieran, I mean."

"Maybe I wasn't," Nola said. "I mean, I thought I was, he was my best friend for forever. I trusted him..."

T squeezed Nola's hand, ignoring the blood on her skin. "You can't always pick who you love."

"It's not supposed to be like this." Anger flushed Nola's cheeks as she said the childish words. "You should be able to love people. To trust people."

"And no one should be hungry, and clean water should fall from the sky," Beauford said.

"How did this happen?" Nola swiped the tears from her cheeks. "How did I end up in a dug out cave with vampires? How did this become the good idea?"

"You got betrayed by a lot of people, and there's nowhere else you can go and stay alive," Beauford said.

"Beauford," T shushed.

"He's right," Nola said. "Living with the devil is better than death."

"See? Start with *better than death* and work your way up from there." Beauford stretched out on the bed.

Footsteps passed in the hall. T sat up straight, staring wide-eyed at the door, but the person on the other side kept walking.

"They'll find him," Nola said.

"They will." T gave a faint smile. "They have to. I came too far to find him."

A minute passed, then another.

"What happens if they can't find him?" T whispered.

"Then you'll still be okay." It was Nola's turn to squeeze T's hand. "You're strong and brave."

"And you're not alone." Beauford spoke with his eyes closed. "Nola and I will be here."

T looked at Nola.

"He's right," Nola said. "We're all here together. And we'll all make sure your baby is safe."

"Thank you."

A cluster of footsteps passed through the hall, the sound rumbling through the door.

Nola wanted to prop open the door to see who was passing by or, better yet, go find Julian and help find Charles herself. But wandering the tunnels would only get her lost.

"What if the baby isn't born healthy?" T whispered. "What if I find Charles, but our baby doesn't survive?"

"Breathe, T," Beauford murmured. "The best thing you can do for the baby is breathe."

"What if the baby hasn't got lungs to breathe or a brain?" T said. "What if the baby already has a terrible disease from my living in the city?"

"Dr. Wynne is the best doctor on the outside," Nola said. "He'll make sure your baby is okay."

Please let Dr. Wynne be able to help her.

Nola held onto T's hand, examining the room to keep from staring at T's belly.

These walls hadn't been carved as smoothly as the walls of the hall. Three bulbs hung from the ceiling, linked together by a red cord that ran through the top of the wall on one side of the room and out the other. There was no window in the room, but the air didn't have the stifling quality she would have expected. Nola searched the walls for the vent pushing in the cool air. Only a four-inch hole in the ceiling gave any hint as to where the air might be coming from.

Emanuel built a good home.

Nola hated herself for being impressed almost as much as she hated herself for being in Nightland.

"Make a count," Beauford said. He'd turned to lie on his side, his brow wrinkling as he watched Nola.

"What do you mean?" Nola asked.

"If you can't decide which is worse, being here or in the domes," Beauford said. "Maybe you're even thinking you would have been better off in the city."

"I wouldn't last a night in the city," Nola said.

"You've had Graylock." T's gaze stayed fixed on the door.

"Okay, a week then," Nola said.

"It's bigger than you surviving, and you know it," Beauford said. "If you want to know who the real monsters are, count bodies. How many has Nightland killed, how many have the domes killed?"

Nola's mind raced through blood and shattered glass. "I don't know all the numbers."

"But you can guess," Beauford said.

"It all changed on the bridge," Nola said. "It would have been Nightland before that."

"But the domes slaughtered wolves and outsiders," Beauford said.

"They were attacking," Nola said.

"The domes attacked Nightland," T said, "and Nightland attacked the domes. And the domes decided to put down the riots and everyone in them, and the wolves decided to fight back. What they put you through on the bridge never should have happened. Outsiders locked up in cages under the domes never should have happened. Needing Vamp to survive never should have happened. Charles leaving me never should have happened. When everything is dark, a lot of *never should have*s happen. This is the only chance we have to survive. They're keeping children alive here. If Nightland will protect my baby, then I don't care who else they've hurt. The domes would have dumped us outside to die at best, killed us themselves if they felt like it. That decides it all for me."

"You're right," Nola whispered. "You're absolutely right."

"There is no right, only the least bloody path to survival." T leaned forward in her chair, staring at the door as though willing it to open.

The room slipped back into silence.

A little girl ran past their door, laughing, and a woman chased her, scolding.

Seventy-two Domers killed when Nightland attacked.

At least a hundred on the bridge when the domes set off the bomb.

She didn't know how many vampires had been killed when the domes had raided Nightland.

Nola gasped as a sharp knock sounded on the door.

"Come in." T tightened her grip on Nola's hand.

Julian stepped into the room, his dark shining hair perfectly in place. His sword sheathed at his hip.

"Nola." He bowed. "It is an unexpected but truly pleasant surprise to see you again." The words rolled perfectly out of his mouth, the inflection different from anyone else Nola had heard speak in the city or the domes.

"I'm just as surprised as you are, Julian," Nola said.

"Julian?" T stood, still clutching Nola's hand. "You're the one who was going to find Charles."

"T?" Julian said.

T nodded.

Nola's heart shattered at the pain that drifted through Julian's black eyes.

"I'm so terribly sorry," Julian said. "I'm afraid Charles didn't make it to our new Nightland."

T's knees buckled. Nola caught her under the arms before she hit the floor.

"What do you mean he didn't make it?" Beauford pushed the chair behind T, helping Nola to lower her into the seat.

"I'm not sure how much you know," Julian said. "Charles came with us to the domes. He was an excellent fighter, one of the best we had."

"Then where is he?" T said.

Nola held onto T, keeping her in the chair even as her whole body shook.

"He was wounded in the fighting at the domes," Julian said. "His group made it out of the glass, but the werewolves had seen the explosion. They were waiting across the bridge. They picked off the wounded before we could stop them. Charles died fighting for a better future for Nightland."

A wail tore from T's throat as she crumpled in Nola's arms.

"I know it won't seem like much now," Julian said, "but Charles wanted Nightland to reach its new home to protect his child. He died ensuring your baby's future. I know he would be happy you found your way to us."

Nola wasn't sure T could understand Julian's words through her sobs.

"You should leave," Beauford said.

"Of course." Julian bowed again. "If there's anything I can do—"

"We need water and food for her," Nola said.

"Right away."

Nola didn't bother to watch the door shut behind him.

Beauford lifted T from her chair.

Nola pulled back the sheets on the nearest cot.

"He's gone," T sobbed. "We came all this way, and he's gone."

Nola pulled up the covers, tucking T in. "Shh, you're okay. We're safe now, and it's going to be okay." She curled up behind T, holding her tightly as she cried. "It's okay. You're going to be okay."

The lie soured in her mouth.

CHAPTER EIGHT

A day had passed. Or maybe only a few hours. It was hard to know when Nola didn't need sleep. Not the way she used to at least.

She made T eat and drink some water. The fruit, bread, and cheese were more than Nola had expected. The water didn't taste of chemicals, or numb her mouth with unknown contamination. A hint of earth was the only thing that set it behind dome standards.

She'd curled up in the same bed with T, holding her while she cried herself to sleep. Beauford snored quietly in the bed across the room. But Nola couldn't sleep. Neither her body nor her brain were tired.

Closing her eyes against the light coming from under the door, she tried to clear her mind. But shadows climbed into her thoughts, unwilling to let her go.

Her mother sitting in her seed laboratory, refusing to acknowledge Nola was gone. Or maybe refusing to admit she'd had a daughter at all. Captain Ridgeway, Jeremy's father and the head of the Outer Guard, pacing in his office, plotting a way to find his son.

Will he be finding him to save him, or to protect the Graylock?

Tears squeezed from Nola's eyes.

It wasn't right. Jeremy shouldn't be out here. He should be safe at home. Raina would have saved Nola.

And I'd be a vampire. And I'd never see Jeremy again.

Nola bit the inside of her lips, willing her tears to stay silent.

The domes would give up on trying to find them soon, if they hadn't already. Even Captain Ridgeway wouldn't risk his men going out beyond the city limits to find his son.

Her tears passed, but still Nola couldn't find sleep.

She'd climbed a mountain, she should be exhausted. She considered each part of her body, from her toes up, looking for pain or strength. Any sign that she had nearly died and chemicals had altered the way her body worked to save her. Everything felt the same.

I'm never going to sleep again.

Nola lifted her arm off of T, hating herself for her choice even as she made it.

The cot squeaked as she stood. Nola froze, waiting for T to wake. But exhaustion and grief trapped her in sleep.

"I'll be back soon," Nola whispered.

Checking the case on her hip, Nola opened the door a crack and slipped out into the hall, closing the door behind her.

"Nola."

She jumped, her heart throttling her throat. She spun to see a boy in jeans and a red shirt sitting on the floor.

"It's just me," Jeremy said as Nola finally looked at his face. "Raina thought it best if I ditched the uniform."

"Probably."

"I feel naked without it." Jeremy stood. The foreign brightness of his shirt didn't diminish his size, but rather made him seem bigger and younger at the same time.

"What are you doing here?" Nola asked.

"I knew you wouldn't be able to sleep." Jeremy shrugged. "And I didn't think you'd want to lie still for very long."

"Do we not sleep?" Nola asked, her head spinning at the concept of never sleeping again. "Does Graylock make it so you can't?"

"You will sleep," Jeremy said. "Just not as much or as often. I only do about six hours every three days."

"Is it awful?"

"Not once you get used to it. Give it a couple weeks and you'll be all right. If we can find you a watch, it'll help. Keeps the meaning in time."

Nola rubbed her eyes, testing them for fatigue. "How did I never notice you not sleeping?" Nola asked. "I slept beside you in your hospital bed. Or was that a lie? Were you only faking?"

"I would never lie to you, Nola."

She made a sound between a growl and a laugh.

"I never lied," Jeremy pressed on. "There were just some things I wasn't allowed to tell you."

"Like that you were taking a drug to change the way your body works or that there was a bomb planted under the bridge?"

"Yes."

Nola turned her back on him, striding down the hall toward Emanuel's library.

"Nola." Jeremy's bootfalls thumped after her. "Nola." He took her arm.

Nola stopped, glaring at Jeremy's hand touching her.

"Sorry." He tucked his hands in his jeans pockets. "I couldn't tell you about Graylock. The whole thing was classified, and the Council had banned normal domes citizens from knowing about it."

"Because sane people would know it was wrong," Nola said.

"But you were willing to forgive it, remember?" A line wrinkled Jeremy's brow. "The Graylock saved me. I would have died without it."

Nola dragged her hand through her hair, catching her fingers on her tangled curls. "Fine, Graylock I can forgive, but using me to kill people—"

"I never thought they'd actually take you out there," Jeremy said, his tone shifting as his desperation grew. "If I had known my dad was going to send you out to face a pack of wolves, I would have told you to hide until it was all over. It wasn't until I saw you by the bridge that I even knew you were there."

"But you knew about the bombs," Nola said. "You knew they were going to wait until the bridge was packed and then blow it up, with both of us still on it."

"Yes. I knew about the bomb."

Nola turned away, unwilling to look at Jeremy's face and see a murderer.

"But I had no control over when the explosives went off." Jeremy stepped around to stand in front of Nola again. "It shouldn't have happened the way it did. They should have blown the bridge as soon as they could. Part of Lucifer's group might have been killed, but it would have been worth it to block the rest of the mob, you've got to be able to see that."

Nola willed her mind back to the bridge. To Lucifer promising to kill and eat the Domers if they wouldn't give up their food supply.

A massacre of the people who hid in the glass castle.

Nola nodded.

"I don't know why my father waited until the bridge was full," Jeremy said. "Maybe he thought you could talk them down, or at least wanted to seem like he'd tried to end things peacefully. Maybe the explosives weren't ready. I don't know. It wasn't my choice. If it had been, you would have stayed inside, and the bridge would have been blown before any Outer Guard set foot on it. I don't know why the guards were ordered to kill you, and I don't know what they would do to me if they found me."

"They'd catch you and stick you in a concrete cell or kill you on sight." Nola wrapped her arms around her chest, trying to squeeze out the pain of thinking of Jeremy dead.

"Nola, when you told me what you'd done to help Nightland, I forgave you."

Nola looked up to the light on the ceiling, willing the brightness to burn away the image of Jeremy's pleading face.

"I was angry, but I knew you were only trying to help people. And those people used you, and lied to you."

"I've been lied to a lot." Nola pushed the words past the knot in her throat.

"I was lied to, too," Jeremy whispered. "The Outer Guard are supposed to protect the citizens of the domes and they used you. They hurt you. I didn't think my father or any of the other guards were capable of that."

"So you want me to just forgive you?" Nola blinked away the spots from the light. Tears trickled down her cheeks. "To just say, 'Oops, I watched a hundred people get blown up, but that's okay, I still love you?'"

"No, I don't." Pain echoed in Jeremy's voice. "I want you to not hate me. I want you to be able to walk next to me without cringing at the sight of me. I need to protect you, Nola."

"I don't need—"

"Because protecting you is all I have. And whether you ever love me again or not, I will spend the rest of my life loving you." He reached out, gently brushing the tears from Nola's cheeks. "I have to keep you safe, because not knowing if you're okay hurts a lot more than getting shot or stabbed, and I don't know if I can take it."

"Jeremy..."

"You don't have to be in love with me," Jeremy said. "But at least trust me to be your friend. I swear to you, Nola, I will never hide anything from you again, even if I think it'll scare you. And no matter what it costs me, I promise there will be no more secrets. Just let me be near you, that's all I need."

"I don't need a bodyguard."

"Then let me teach you to fight," Jeremy said. "Since I've promised honesty, it felt really good to see you pummeling Kieran."

Nola coughed a laugh.

"But your form was bad." Jeremy grinned. "You could have done a lot more damage if you knew what you were doing."

A twinkle glimmered in the corner of his eye. Like the old Jeremy, the one who had always known how to make her laugh, was waiting right below the surface.

Either way it'll hurt.

"Fine," Nola said. "You can teach me how to fight. But you don't get to fight for me, or speak for me, or make choices for me."

"Deal." Jeremy held out his hand.

"Deal."

The warmth of Jeremy's hand spread up Nola's arm. It would be so easy to twine her fingers through his. To lean into his chest and feel safe and secure, like being so far from home didn't matter because home had come with her.

"It's probably best we're on speaking terms anyway." She dropped Jeremy's hand but let him keep step beside her as they continued toward the library. "I have no idea what Graylock is doing to me, we're the only two on Graylock outside the domes' control, and the only two Domers in Nightland."

"It'll be good to have you watching my back," Jeremy said. "I have a feeling the Vampers will be a lot friendlier to you than they will to me."

A smile curved Nola's lips before she could stop it. "First rule: don't call them Vampers. Go with vampires. It's more likely to keep their teeth from your neck."

"I'm learning already."

The doors to Emanuel's library were shut. Nola had never been left on her own to wander the tunnels of Nightland under the city. She'd only been alone as she fled the blood and screams of the Outer Guard's attack on the club. She raised her hand to knock. Flakes of blood still marked her knuckles.

She shoved the doors open. Her heart skipped a beat as she waited for someone to scream at her for barging in or to attack her for being in a forbidden place.

But the library was empty and unguarded.

"What are we doing here?" Jeremy asked. "Not that I'm questioning your decision."

"In the tunnels, Dr. Wynne's laboratory was right behind the library, in Emanuel's house. We need to see Dr. Wynne, and this seems like a good place to look."

A painting hung over the door at the back of the room. Nola studied the picture as they neared. A girl in a garden, sitting in a sea of flowers, surrounded by trees dripping with fruit.

Emanuel's dream for Eden.

Nola paused with her hand on the door. To enter the throne room was one thing, to enter a home another.

Knock, knock, knock.

The sound thudded through the thick door.

The door swung open a few seconds later.

Raina, her hair re-dyed to its scarlet and purple streaked glory, leaned against the doorjamb. "Have you come to punch Kieran some more?"

"He would deserve it if I had," Nola said.

"Aren't children adorable with their little temper tantrums?" Raina cooed.

"We're here to see Dr. Wynne," Nola said. "I'm assuming his lab is back here."

"Keep the jewels close to the keeper." Raina stepped out of their way. "Be gentle with the doctor."

"How is he?" Nola asked.

"His eyes are turning a nice shade of black." Raina led them down the hall, past a kitchen and four closed doors.

"He had to take ReVamp?" Grief pressed into Nola's lungs.

"His genius bordering on madness had turned more to madness," Raina said. "His memory started to slip when Kieran was almost killed by the Outer Guard who raided Nightland."

"And what good is he to Emanuel without his brain?" Nola said.

"What good is he to himself if he can't think?" Raina said. "He injected himself, no one pinned him down."

"At least there's some mercy in that," Jeremy said.

"Oh, are we letting lover boy speak?" Raina stopped at the only metal door in the hall.

"My name is Jeremy."

"So says you." Raina tapped on the door, not waiting before she swung it open. "Company, Doctor."

"Company?" Dr. Wynne looked up from the papers on his desk. His hair had gone fully gray and stuck out at odd angles, as though each of his thoughts blew his hair in a new direction. His pale skin had been nearly translucent the last time Nola had seen him, but the ReVamp had thickened it, hiding the trails of blue. The drugs had begun turning his eyes black, but as they found Nola's face, they held a sharper awareness than Nola had seen from him in a very long time.

"Magnolia." The doctor was on his feet in an instant, crossing the lab in a few strides to pull Nola into a hearty hug. "I'm so happy you're safe."

"Dr. Wynne," Jeremy said.

Dr. Wynne let go of Nola. "Jeremy Ridgeway. I thought Kieran must have made a mistake when he said you were here." Dr. Wynne shook his head and Jeremy's hand. "Well, as surprised as I am that you've sought refuge here, I'm glad you made it in one piece."

"Thank you." A hint of something between fear and disgust flitted through Jeremy's eyes as he looked at Dr. Wynne.

"You'll both be assets to Nightland, of course." Dr. Wynne

smiled, either not noticing or not caring about Jeremy's coldness. "There is so much work to be done. The gardens are still expanding, and so many vampires are undisciplined. You need discipline to be prepared to defend your home."

"You also need discipline if you're going to invade someone else's." Jeremy spoke through clenched teeth.

"Actually"—Nola stepped in front of Jeremy—"we were hoping you might be able to help us."

"Help you?" Dr. Wynne squinted at Nola's face. "You don't appear to be ill."

"I'm not." Nola opened the black case at her hip, pulling free one precious syringe. "But only because this saved me." She held the black liquid up to the light.

CHAPTER NINE

"Will you thank Dr. Wynne again for me?" T's soft voice bounced off the stone walls of the corridor.

"Of course," Julian said.

T, Beauford, and Nola clustered around him as he strode down the hall, Jeremy trailing ten feet behind. "He is the best doctor Nightland has to offer. And quite frankly, I think it was a relief for him to do something as joyful as check on a mother and baby. A nice change from other tasks."

Like finding a way to make more Graylock. Nola chewed on her bottom lip.

"And it'll be a nice change to get all of you outside as well. I'm sure it'll be quite healthy," Julian pressed on. "Dr. Wynne recommends it, and I must say my own mother would have thought the same." Julian led them down a flight of roughly hewn stone steps. "A task to perform. Something important to do."

Fresh air wafted up from below.

"Of course, I won't pretend we don't need the help. Especially from you, Nola. We don't have anyone as qualified in botany as you are."

The stairs ended at a doorway to the open air. Two different doors had been left ajar. One with thick metal bars like a cage, the other solid metal like the door through which they had entered the mountain.

"Of course, I don't know if there's anything that truly requires your specialty to be done this evening, and Kieran has been doing an excellent job of maintaining the gardens," Julian said.

Jeremy took a few quick strides, catching up to Nola and walking right behind her shoulder.

"We wouldn't be able to maintain our non-vampire population without him," Julian said. "But when resources are scarce, every innovation possible is needed to produce food."

"Happy to help," Nola said. "Is everything set up the way it was in Nightland, or have..."

The rest of her question faded from her mind as they reached the open air.

They hadn't arrived in another brief opening before a new set of tunnels, but in a valley carved out between the peaks of the mountains.

Terraces had been cut into the slopes, creating steps of soil supporting rows of crops. Disks of fabric, larger than any Nola had ever seen, had been placed around the tops of the mountain. Though the half-moon gave the only light, Nola could imagine the parasol-like fabric blocking out the worst rays of the sun.

Julian led them to the far side of the narrow valley toward the steps that cut up the terraces.

"How do you block the rain?" Nola asked.

"We don't usually need to." Kieran wound his way through a row of greens, dirt coating his clothes.

Nola's hands instinctively curled into fists as he stopped in front of their group.

"The pollution that causes the acid rain usually stays pretty low over the city," Kieran said. "Most of the rain at this elevation is clean. And when it looks like we might get bad rain, we cover everything by hand. I'd love to have a tenting system, but keeping the sun from scorching the crops had to be the first priority."

"Good evening, Kieran," Julian said. "I've brought four more to help with the gardens."

Kieran looked to Nola. "I need all the help I can get."

"It looks like you've done well all on your own," Nola said. "This is huge compared to the garden on the roof above Nightland in the city. Were you running up to the mountains to plant things on off days? Why did you even bother taking the plants you'd been working with in the city when you had so much here? You could have left them behind. People could still be eating from that garden."

The people working in the rows around them stood, watching Nola as she shouted.

She couldn't bring herself to care. "What the hell did you need from the domes if you have all this out here?"

"Nola, I don't know if this is the venue for a lovers' quarrel," Julian said.

"Maybe we should go dig something," Beauford said.

"We have less than twenty crops we can grow out here, Nola," Kieran said. "Do the math. That isn't sustainable. Bugs, bacteria, we could lose everything, and people would starve. The domes aren't the only ones planning for the future."

Jeremy stepped forward to stand next to Nola. "When plans involve killing people, they're usually bad plans."

"Weren't you an Outer Guard?" Kieran asked. "Did you get through that without hurting anyone?"

The gardeners crept closer, whether for entertainment or to defend Kieran, Nola didn't know.

"Just tell us what work you want us to do." Beauford pointed to a barrel holding shovels, hoes, and rakes. "Let's stop talking and shovel things."

"What did you take?" Nola asked. "What did you need that

you couldn't ask for in the trade? Remember the time you traded me for seeds and medicine? What was so precious the domes wouldn't pay it to get me back?"

"They would have paid anything," Jeremy said. "Between your mother and my father, there's nothing the Council wouldn't have given to get you back safely. I was waiting outside the meeting with the ice from the Graylock taking over my veins. I heard it all. The domes would have done anything to get her back."

Nola laid her hand on Jeremy's arm. He stopped shaking at her touch.

"What did you steal, Kieran?" Nola asked.

Kieran looked up at the stars. "You'll have to ask Emanuel. I was only a guide to get them in and out as quickly as possible while meeting as few guards as possible. I was trying to keep as many people safe as I could."

"By betraying your home?" Jeremy said.

"The domes kicked me out," Kieran said. "Nightland is my home. Nightland saved me and my father. Nightland took care of us when the domes left us outside to die."

"Kieran—"

He spoke over Nola. "I didn't know when we gave you back that Emanuel needed more from the domes before we could leave the city. I couldn't stop the raid, so I went to the domes to try and get in and out as fast as we could. If the vampires who went in hadn't known exactly where to go, how many more people would have died? Did I really do something so terrible?"

"Yes!" Jeremy spat.

"You told them not to hurt me," Nola said. "You led them into my home. You let them kill people all around me, but I had to survive."

"I couldn't let them touch you." Kieran spoke softly. "It was the only protection I could give you, and the thought of anyone hurting you is more than I can stand."

"It wasn't mercy." Nola dug her nails into her palms, refusing to let tears come. "And it wasn't kindness. And it didn't work anyway. I got bit, Kieran. Raina saved me, not you."

"Who bit you?" Kieran said. "Tell me who it was and—"

"And what?" Nola asked. "You'll kill him?"

"Nola, I'm so sorry." Pain creased Kieran's face.

"Can we just work on the garden? It would be a lot more useful than apologies." Nola studied the nearest greenery, unwilling to look at Kieran any longer. Leaves from a potato plant peeked up through the dirt.

"We have some squash ready to harvest down the row," Kieran said, his voice even and unreadable. "We're almost to the end of what we can grow out here for the season. With the nights getting cold, there's not much we can keep alive."

"And then what do people eat?" Beauford asked.

"What we've stored, and what we can grow below," Kieran said. "I want to build a way to grow in the cold season aboveground, but that will have to wait until next year."

"Just don't try stealing glass from the domes." Jeremy moved out in front of their group. "The guards would destroy you."

"There's plenty of glass to salvage in the city." Kieran stepped forward. "Just because the domes demand fancy glass doesn't mean it's the only way things can work."

"Nola, I'm sure you're up to harvesting some squash," Julian said loudly. "Why don't you lead Beauford and T down that way? I'm sure Kieran has work to get back to, and Jeremy can help me transfer the new soil from below."

"I should stay with Nola." Jeremy's fiery gaze stayed on Kieran.

"I can harvest some plants without supervision." Nola stalked down the row, her brain pounding with all the things she wanted to scream.

The path ended before the edge of the slope, blocking the area beyond with a fence. Edges cut through the soil and grass, the first round of digging to build more steps for growing. Goats wandered through the grass, grazing without caring for the vampires working nearby.

"Nola."

She jumped at T's quiet voice.

"Just pick the dull-colored ones with no green." Nola knelt next to the long, prickly vine.

"The squash in the domes were bigger." T began lowering herself to the ground, pain wrinkling the corners of her eyes.

"Careful." Beauford took her arm, helping her the rest of the way.

"Is it the baby?" Nola asked.

"No, I just climbed a mountain." T's smile lasted for only a second. "Are you all right?"

"I'm fine." Nola's stomach twisted. "Please don't worry about me."

"Better than worrying about me." T took Nola's hand. "You're going through a lot, being asked to forgive a lot."

"I just..." Nola grabbed a heavy gourd, twisting the vine until it broke. "I just don't know if some things should be forgiven."

"Some shouldn't," T said. "Maybe there have been too many lies, and too much blood spilt, and too much hurt to ever forgive." T reached to twist a squash free.

Beauford moved her hands, doing the work for her.

"The thing is"—T sat back on her heels—"I had this whole speech planned for when I found Charles. I was so mad that he left me behind to go fight with Nightland. He left me alone in a city on the edge of burning itself to the ground with no way to keep a baby safe. And then he didn't come back when he was supposed to be right home. And I had to go to the domes, and be locked in a cell, and break out, and I shouldn't have had to do any of it." Tears streamed down T's face. "He should have stayed in the apartment with me, and waited for whatever Nightland was doing to be done. Then he should have brought me here himself. I was going to scream at the top of my lungs if I had to, to make sure he understood all the things he had done that had hurt me. And now he's dead."

"I'm so sorry." Nola wrapped her arm around T's shoulders.

"He's dead, and I still want to scream at him. But I would go through the hell he left me in all over again to see him alive. I'm not saying you have to forgive them, Nola." T took Nola's face in her hands. "I don't know if what they've done is so horrible forgiveness is impossible. Maybe you can't ever love either of them again, and that's your choice. But at least you have a choice. You can decide if you forgive them or love them or never want to see them again. I would do anything to have that."

Nola hugged T tightly. She didn't know what words to use to say how grateful she was T had come into the domes to work and trusted Nola enough to follow her out.

"Think about it, Nola," T whispered. "Think about what you really want."

"How?" Nola sat in the dirt, studying the terraces.

Kieran worked three rows below, digging up plants that had passed for the season. Jeremy and Julian were nowhere in sight.

"I barely know where I am." Nola pinched a vine with her fingers and spilt the rough fibers apart. It should have been hard, tearing at her skin and making her wish she had a knife to do the job. But the vine snapped without her really having to try. "I don't know what I'm capable of, or turning into. How am I supposed to choose?"

"Choose between Kieran and Jeremy?" Beauford lifted the squash Nola had split from the vine. "Who says you have to? You're strong and capable. You'll be just fine on your own."

"You really think so?" Nola asked.

"Got out of the domes without either of them, didn't you? Catlyn always used to say, 'Never need someone more than you love them.'" Beauford's smile didn't reach his eyes. "You don't need anyone. If you decide to love someone, that's your choice. But you don't have to. The world is ending. The only mandatory thing is survival."

CHAPTER TEN

The simple tasks of working in the garden helped. Laboring side-by-side with T and Beauford felt normal. Like they were back in the safety of the domes. Nola's shoulders relaxed as she made her way down the row. Dirt clumped under her nails, giving her hands the familiar look of productivity she knew so well from her years harvesting in the domes. Years spent feeding people who now wanted her dead.

Tension crept back into Nola's shoulders.

She focused instead on the people around her. T and Beauford worked as a team, Beauford never letting T lift anything. Part of Nola wanted to tell T to go rest, but most of her knew better. Sitting alone in a room with nothing but time and grief would do more damage than kneeling in the dirt.

Jeremy and Julian had gone back into the tunnels and had yet to return. Kieran worked at the base of the terraces, placing tall metal stakes into the unplanted ground. Strangers worked around them as well.

A woman with dark green eyes mingled with the goats as they chewed their way through the grass beyond the fence. On the terraces facing Nola, fruit trees hid beneath the disks of fabric.

An older man wove his way between the trees, inspecting the progress of their bounty.

Kieran had done a wonderful job.

My mother would be proud.

Or disgusted.

Orange touched the sky, burning the night away.

"We should start heading in," Nola said.

T looked up at the sky. "I've been out in the sun before."

"But you shouldn't be, none of us should," Nola said.

"It's so easy for Domers to say things like that." Beauford stood, brushing his hands off on his pants. "But if it's let the sun bite your skin or starve, you can live through the rays well enough."

"But it isn't live through the sun or starve," Julian said. "Not here."

Carrying an empty crate in each hand, he walked up the row toward them. Jeremy followed behind, more crates perched on his shoulders.

"We work at night," Julian said, "which means our work day is ending. If you'll put the fruits of your labor into these, we can get inside."

Beauford took a crate from Julian and passed it to Nola, then took Jeremy's extra for himself.

Nola carried her box to the end of the row.

A goat hollered at her as she carefully placed the squash in the bin.

"These aren't for you," Nola said. "I doubt you'd even eat the leaves anyway."

It took only a few minutes for her to fill her bin. She stared down at the loaded crate. In the domes, everything would have been placed on a wheeled cart.

"Do you want help?" T asked.

"No," Nola said.

Julian and Jeremy had both moved their crates to the bottom

of the terrace. Beauford had hoisted his up. His muscles strained the fabric of his sleeves as he carried his load down the steps.

Jeremy looked up at Nola. Without saying a word, he started up the stairs toward her.

"It won't do any harm to let him help," T said.

"I can do it myself." Nola crouched next to the crate. There were no handles to grab onto. Her only choice was to get her fingers under the bottom.

"Nola." Jeremy jogged down the row.

She shoved her fingers under the bottom and lifted. She waited for pain to shoot through her fingers, or her balance to sway at the weight. But the crate lifted like it weighed no more than it had empty.

"Careful." Jeremy stopped in front of her, his hands reaching for the crate.

"It doesn't feel like it weighs anything." Nola shifted the weight back and forth in her arms.

"Don't push it," Jeremy warned.

"It has to be, what, sixty pounds? It doesn't feel like anything."

"The Graylock is working," Jeremy said.

"If this is how Graylock is supposed to work, why are you telling me to be careful?" Nola narrowed her eyes.

"I kept breaking things my first few days." A hint of pink crept up Jeremy's cheeks. "I destroyed about five doorframes before I relearned how to close doors."

"I'm sure your dad loved that," Nola laughed. The bounce of it loosened the pain in her chest.

"He wasn't too mad." Jeremy stepped aside, letting Nola and T pass, then followed them down the row. "He'd had a whole pack of guards breaking things for a while. Your mom freaked when I broke the door to your house."

Nola turned at the edge of the steps. "You broke a door in my house?"

"Yeah." Jeremy ran a hand over his closely cropped hair.

"When you were out for a couple of days. Your mom made maintenance fix it right away. She didn't want you to feel like your home had been broken."

Tension gripped Nola's jaw. "Our home was broken. A door wouldn't have made it any worse."

"I—" All hint of laughter faded from Jeremy's face. "Nola, I'm sorry."

"For breaking a door?" Nola walked down the stairs. "Don't be. You took the medicine to try and help me. You broke a door when you were worried about me. I just can't believe my mother's priorities were so skewed, and the domes went along with her."

"But at least she noticed the door was broken." Jeremy leapt down a few steps to walk by Nola's side. "The whole thing is too messed up to riddle through, but at least in all the chaos, and your mother freaking out about protecting the seeds, she took a minute to worry about you. Maybe she was worrying about the wrong thing, but she noticed something and cared enough to fix it."

"This way, if you will." Julian gave one last glance to the rising sun and headed toward the tunnel.

The gardens were nearly empty. Only the green-eyed woman with the goats remained outside.

"Do you think they hate us now?" Nola asked.

"Close the door behind you, if you please," Julian called from the front of the line.

"What about the woman outside?" T squeezed to the back of the group, leaning with all her weight to close the metal door. Locks clicked into place as soon as the door shut.

"She'll be out until nightfall," Julian said. "Don't worry, it's her own choice to stay with her precious goats. It's a rather strange affinity she has for them, but the goats are healthy and breeding like mad, so we find it best to let her be."

"Ha." Beauford's monosyllabic laugh echoed off the walls.

"Nola, who do you think hates us?" Jeremy asked.

The tunnel widened as they reached the main level.

"Our families," Nola whispered.

"I don't know," Jeremy said. "The best we can hope is that they've given us up for dead."

Nola tightened her grip on the bin, the wood cracked in protest.

"Careful," Jeremy said.

"The best we can hope for is that they're comforting themselves that we're dead," Nola said. "We're their children."

"Children who ran away from the domes," Jeremy said. "They spent time and a ton of resources raising and training us."

Julian turned left into a side corridor, which slanted down, cutting deeper into the mountain.

We're a waste of resources.

"What's the worst?" Nola asked.

"Huh?" Jeremy stepped behind Nola as their path narrowed.

"If us being dead is the best, what's the worst?"

"They're considering us rogue assets," Jeremy said. "They know our training. They know how useful we both are, and they don't want anyone else to have us. You know enough about botany to help build greenhouses out here that could produce enough food to allow the humans of Nightland to thrive. I'm a trained Outer Guard who knows all the domes' security procedures. And all that's without us having Graylock."

"Is that why they wanted me dead?" The words didn't sting as much as she thought they would. "Not because they wanted to punish me for the crime of helping people escape, but because if they couldn't have me no one could?"

"Yeah," Jeremy said, "which made my leaving a really easy decision."

A wide door blocked the end of the corridor.

Julian balanced his bin on his hip and knocked with his free hand. "Produce from the garden."

Nola waited for a voice to call back through the wood.

Julian peered into his bin, as though checking the squash for instantaneous spoilage as the seconds ticked past.

"Should we just go in?" Nola asked.

Julian looked up from his crate as the door swung slowly open. An old woman peeked her head out.

"Bea?" Nola stepped forward, recognizing the woman's wrinkled face. "You used to work in Emanuel's house. You cared for Eden."

"We all care for Eden." Julian slipped through the door. "And all of this is Emanuel's house."

Bea stayed in the doorway, glancing into each of their bins as they passed.

"It's good to see you again," Nola said. She forgot to listen for an answer as she entered the room beyond.

Wooden barrels lined the walls. Dried herbs and meat hung from lines above. Tables laden with food took up the center of the space. On the far wall, rows upon rows of glass jars filled ceiling-high shelves, surrounding a smaller door, which stood ajar. The scents of smoke, meat, and hot sugar drifted from the room beyond.

"What is this place?" T reached for the apples lined up on one of the tables.

Bea slapped her hand away.

"The pantry," Julian said, "and it is controlled by the fiercest woman in all of Nightland. So best to leave the crates on the floor and be on our way."

Bea peered into each of their crates as they placed them on the ground then stared at them until they were through the door and safely in the corridor.

"How long have the gardens here been growing?" Nola asked.

"This is the first full season." Julian led them back up the way they'd come. "We'd been trying to farm up here for quite a while, but with little success. Kieran's plans for the garden changed things. Without his insight, we wouldn't be able to feed our non-blood drinkers."

"But he was in the city," Nola said. "I saw him."

"He had been here when he took ill," Julian said. "We barely got him to his father in time for the ReVamp to be effective. After that, Dr. Wynne refused to be separated from his son, and the doctor's presence was required in the city."

"To care for Eden," Nola said. "Where is she?"

"Safe," Julian said, "healthy, and turning out to be a very bright little girl."

"Good." Pictures of the tiny girl with big dark eyes flitted through Nola's mind.

"How long did it take to build this place?" Jeremy ran his finger along the stone wall. "You said you've been harvesting for a season. This construction took a lot more than a year."

"Quite right." Julian headed down the main corridor that led to the room Nola shared with Beauford and T. "The expansion to the natural cave system began years ago. Long before I found my way to this corner of the world. It took a long time to build our true Nightland, but I have to believe it was worth every year of labor and hardship to have a place to reimagine the future of those fighting for survival in this world."

"I thought Nightland was the tunnels under the city?" Beauford said.

"Nightland is a people not a place," Julian said. "We were Nightland in the city, and now we are Nightland here."

They stopped in front of the door marked 113.

"What would have happened if the tunnels up here weren't ready yet?" Nola hung back as T and Beauford went into their room, both slumping with fatigue.

"We wouldn't have come here," Julian said. "If we had attempted the transition before everything was ready, the endeavor would have failed."

"But if the domes had gone after Nightland a little sooner,"

Nola said, "or if the city had eaten itself alive, what would have happened then?"

"We would all have died," Julian said. "Whether here or in the city. There would have been no hope for long term survival."

"What I don't get is how you pulled it off," Jeremy said. "This wasn't done by Vampers—"

"Vampires," Nola hushed.

"—with pickaxes," Jeremy finished.

"It was built by the architects," Julian said. "They spent years on our home, and now they've moved on to building another refuge for another group. They're working nearly a continent away from what I understand."

"The architects? Who are they?" Jeremy asked. "Why did they decide to build here?"

"Emanuel is very old, has lived a life of many marvels, and is owed many debts," Julian said. "There are some debts that can't be repaid even by building a village under a mountain."

Nola shuddered at the mere thought of what debt could be so great.

"They just travel and build?" Jeremy crossed his arms, his eyes narrowed. "So, you're saying there are other settlements hiding underground?"

"Most definitely. And not all of them were built by the architects," Julian said. "I've heard of a settlement out west in a long forgotten military shelter. The people who built the domes found the structure to be unappealing for their purposes, but that doesn't mean the space can't aid in survival."

"That's a lot of people," Nola said. "I thought it was only the domes that could survive."

"Of course that's what you were taught." Julian smiled kindly. "Swearing allegiance to the domes is much simpler if they are the only available path. There are many truths the domes have dismissed. Too many to be discussed this morning. Rest, both of you. I'm sure I can rattle your world views a bit more when the sun sets."

Julian gave each of them a nod and headed down the hall, leaving Nola to stew in her thoughts.

"They lied to us," Nola said. "The domes must know."

"They don't know about this place, and it's right on their doorstep." Jeremy dug the heels of his hands into his eyes. "Are you tired yet?"

"No," Nola said. "I wish I were. I wish I could fall asleep and forget about the mess my life has turned into."

"I have a better idea." A hint of a smile played at the corners of Jeremy's lips.

"What?"

"Your strength from the Graylock is kicking in," Jeremy said. "Want to go test it out? I'll teach you to throw a proper punch."

Nola bit the insides of her cheeks, willing her face to stay passive. "No time like the present to learn to defend myself."

CHAPTER ELEVEN

The sparring room hadn't been cleared out by the rising of the sun.

A few had taken refuge in the cots along the side of the space. A man with his teeth filed into sharp fangs slept with his mouth dangling open, though Nola didn't understand how anyone could sleep through all the noise in the room.

Pairs matched up in the squares painted on the floor.

One pair sparred with staffs, while the match next to them was fought with swords. The center four blocks had been taken over by a group of six, who had no weapons but their own hands.

Vampires stood around the periphery, cheering and stomping their feet as the fight heated up.

A girl no older than Nola with bright blond hair dove into the middle of the fight, kicking a man twice her size in the stomach with enough force to send him flying out of their squares.

The bystanders laughed and jeered as the man hit the ground. Two women grabbed him under the arms, throwing him back into the fight. He hit a younger man in the back, knocking him over.

The blond girl twisted the larger man's arm behind his back with a knee to his neck, pinning him to the ground.

"We're not going to be doing that, right?" Nola asked. "I don't think I'm ready for that."

The young man knocked the blond girl aside, dragging the fallen man to his feet only to punch him in the face and knock him over again.

"No," Jeremy said. "We aren't going to brawl."

"Good. Not brawling is good." Nola kept close on his heels as they moved toward an open square on the far side of the room.

"We're going to start nice and slow." Jeremy stopped in the center of a green square. "Just how to throw a proper punch."

"Is that how they start the guards?" Nola asked.

"Kind of," Jeremy said. "First, they run you till you feel like you can't breathe anymore. Then it's strength training until you can't lift your arms anymore. Then you learn how to hit things."

"But I don't have to run until I can't breathe?"

"You've already had Graylock." Jeremy rolled up his sleeves. "Honestly, we could run through the tunnels for a couple of hours to see if you get winded, and go lift some barrels for strength, but I'd rather you learn to defend yourself. Just in case...well, in case you need to."

"To punch a vampire?" Nola asked.

"Or someone on Graylock," Jeremy said. "You should be able to defend yourself against everyone."

Nola grinned, the expression slipping too easily onto her face. "What should we be called? If people who take Lycan are were-wolves, and people on Vamp and ReVamp are vampires, what does that make us?"

"Superheroes." Laughter glimmered in Jeremy's eyes.

"Okay, Captain Domer, how do I punch things?" Nola widened her stance, planting her hands on her hips.

"Not things," Jeremy laughed. "People. Punching is only for people."

"Can you imagine Pillion teaching self-defense in school?" A laugh bubbled up from Nola's throat. *"Punching is for People and Other Basics."*

Tears streamed down Nola's cheeks as Jeremy gave a comical frown, looking shockingly like Mr. Pillion himself. "Your skin and bones will never be stronger than stone or metal. Punching is a skill only useful for defense against assault by other people. If a wall or a door is attacking, kicking is a much more useful tactic."

Nola brushed the tears off her cheeks. "No wonder they never taught us any of this in school. None of us would have been able to take it seriously."

"They should have though." The joy vanished from Jeremy's face. "They should have made all of us learn to defend ourselves and basic first aid. If they had, things would have gone differently when Nightland attacked. They're just too cocky. Living safely behind the glass and assuming nothing can hurt them. Not the sun, or rain, or thousands of desperate people. How could they have been so stupid?"

"They." The word rushed from Nola's lungs, stealing all the air from her.

"What?"

"You said *they*." Nola looked up to the stone ceiling, so different from what she had grown up with in the domes. "They and them. That's what you said. Not us and we."

"We aren't them," Jeremy said. "Not anymore. It's just us, Nola."

"Two superheroes alone in the world?"

The clattering of the fighting around them drilled into her ears, shaking her breath as she exhaled.

"The only ones of our kind. Then I'd better learn to fight," Nola said. "You can't do all the fighting. I have to be able to pull my weight or we won't survive."

"Then punch me." Jeremy held up his hands. "Go on, punch."

"Just punch your hand?" Nola glanced around. All the other pairs were sparring full force. Heat crept up her cheeks.

"Come on," Jeremy said. "Don't think about it."

Nola drew back her hand and punched, hitting Jeremy's palm.

"Okay," Jeremy said. "That's a good start, but don't pull your arm back. If someone sees you prep, they'll know exactly what you're trying to do. Keep your hands in front of you."

"Okay." She balled her hands into fists, holding them in front of her chest.

"And don't put your thumbs on the inside your fists." Jeremy took Nola's hands, moving her thumbs to sit safely on the outside of her fingers. "Now try it again."

Nola punched again, hitting the tips of Jeremy's fingers.

"Try for—"

"Aiming?" Nola cut him off, striking the middle of his palm.

"Good." Jeremy nodded. "But even as strong as you are, you've got to put the force of your body into it. Use your shoulders to rotate—"

"Nola, if you want to learn to fight, you could ask someone who's actually good at it." Raina sauntered into the green square.

Kieran hovered outside the lines, a knife in each hand.

"The child was a guard for what, a weekend?" Raina asked.

"Jeremy knows what he's doing," Nola said.

"Show me." Raina tipped her head, her hair shimmering as it swished to the side.

"Okay." Nola squared off to Jeremy and punched his palm again.

Raina tossed her head back and laughed. "I take it back lover boy, keep her until she gets past Kindergarten."

"At least I'm trying to learn." Nola pulled her fist back and punched again.

"Not like that." Kieran stepped forward, his eyes darting from Jeremy to Nola. "You have to keep your wrist straight. If you let it tip to the side, you'll break your wrist. It doesn't matter how fast you can heal, broken bones still suck."

"I can teach her to throw a punch," Jeremy said. "Try it again, Nola."

"She's going to break her wrist if she keeps going like that." Kieran stepped forward.

"And I'll make sure she doesn't." The muscles in Jeremy's neck tensed, forming root-like ridges. "The only time she's ever thrown a punch is at your face. I'm starting her from the beginning."

"I'm just trying to help," Kieran said.

"She doesn't need your help," Jeremy said.

"Don't speak for me," Nola said softly.

Raina let out a low whistle.

"Nola, do you want to break your wrist, or do you want my help?" Kieran said.

"I'll make sure she doesn't get hurt," Jeremy said. "I'm the trained guard, not you."

"And dome training is the best?" Kieran said. "Have you seen the vampires of Nightland fight hand to hand? Outer Guard rely on trucks and guns and things we don't have out here. If she wants to survive, she's going to have to do it the Nightland way."

"I can teach her. I can keep her safe." Red had taken over Jeremy's cheeks.

"You're not the only one who wants to protect her," Kieran said.

"And what a great job you did!" Jeremy flung his arms wide, stepping toward Kieran. "She snuck out into the city because of you. Because you lured her out there."

"I never wanted—"

"Never wanted what?" Jeremy spat. "To steal her I-Vent? To convince her to steal from the domes? You almost got her killed!"

"To be fair," Raina said, "I'm the one who actually stabbed her."

"Nola can handle herself," Kieran said. "She's stronger than you give her credit for."

"Then let me learn to punch people!" Nola stepped between Kieran and Jeremy.

The boys stared at each other.

"I'll be happy to keep teaching you," Jeremy said.

"I don't know if you're the best person for the job," Kieran said.

"I have an idea." Raina took Nola's shoulders, pulling her outside the green square. "You both want to teach Nola, and no one can agree on who's the more qualified. So let's have a demonstration."

"Raina, no," Nola said.

Raina ignored her. "No better way to see who's the better teacher than finding out who's the better fighter. It's not like you two don't want to beat the hell out of each other, and I could use the entertainment besides."

"Raina, this is a terrible idea."

Jeremy and Kieran glowered at each other.

"They don't have to if they don't want to." Raina grinned.

Kieran tossed his knives on the floor. "You want to hit me, fine. Give it your best shot, and we'll see how well that Graylock of yours actually works."

"A lot better than ReVamp. I can still walk in the sun." Jeremy took a step to the side.

Kieran matched him, moving in the opposite direction.

"See? They wanted to fight," Raina whispered. "They're prowling like angry kittens. It's cute."

Nola balled her hands into fists as they kept circling each other.

"My father created ReVamp without any of the fancy resources the domes have. He's the only hope you have for getting more Graylock."

"Then I hope he's up to the task." Jeremy charged forward, plowing his shoulder into Kieran's ribs.

Kieran kicked out, catching Jeremy behind the knee and sending him stumbling to the side.

"What if he's not?" Kieran said. "What if he can't replicate it? What if you gave Nola something you don't have more of?"

"We have enough to finish her dose."

"And then we just hope no one tries to kill her?" Kieran darted forward, punching Jeremy in the jaw and ribs, then catching him in the chin with his elbow.

Jeremy stumbled back.

Kieran lunged to strike again, but Jeremy blocked the blow, hitting Kieran hard in the stomach.

"I'll keep her safe." Jeremy wiped the blood from the corner of his mouth.

"She would have been safer with ReVamp," Kieran said. "Even you've got to know that. Better supply, being a part of the strongest group the outside has. You made a mistake."

Jeremy charged forward, fists raised.

Kieran swung, but Jeremy ducked, dodging the blow. Jeremy kicked low, knocking Kieran's legs out from under him. Kieran hit the ground hard.

"I saved her life," Jeremy growled.

"Raina could have done it." In one fluid movement, Kieran sprang to his feet. "She could have given Nola the ReVamp. Did you not think, or are you just that selfish?"

"She was bleeding out," Jeremy said. "I had Graylock on me, and I saved her life. You know who wasn't there to give his opinion? You."

Kieran jumped five feet into the air, launching himself at Jeremy and bringing his elbow down on Jeremy's shoulder with a sickening *crunch*.

Jeremy stumbled back, sweat slicking his brow.

"Your precious guards were trying to kill her," Kieran said.

"And I made sure they didn't." Jeremy ran forward, knocking Kieran to the ground, pinning him down with his knees pressed into his chest. "When your precious Vampers blew up part of the domes, it was me who took care of her. You weren't there to wash the blood out of her hair." He sank his knuckles into Kieran's eye. "You weren't the one who held her when she was sobbing like she would break apart." He hit again. "She was bleeding in the middle of the street." He struck again. "She wouldn't open her eyes. I thought she was gone."

He sprang to his feet, lifting Kieran with him. Kieran didn't fight as Jeremy slammed him to the ground.

"I've made some mistakes," Jeremy said. "Graylock wasn't one. Nola's breathing. If you don't like how I did it, go walk in the sun."

The air went still. The ones sparring around them had stopped. All eyes were on Jeremy.

Raina clapped, the sound bouncing off the stone walls. "Now wasn't that therapeutic?"

"Don't." Jeremy ran his hands over his hair. Blood marked his knuckles. His eyes met Nola's. "I just..." He shook his head. Without another word, he turned and stalked back toward the tunnels, ignoring the stares of everyone he passed.

"Kieran," Nola said. "Are you okay?"

He rolled onto his back. Bruises covered his face, and blood trickled from his nose.

"Kieran?"

"Whose blood was in your hair?"

"What?" Nola stepped closer.

The vampires around them had lost interest in the green square. *Clangs* of weapons and *thumps* of fists rumbled around the cavern.

"He said there was blood in your hair. Whose was it?"

"I don't know." Nola stood over Kieran. "Mine, the man I killed, probably some other people's. I don't remember all of it. I don't think I want to."

"We never should have sent you back." Kieran sat up, wincing as he moved. "You wanted to stay with Nightland. Emanuel should have let you."

"And what, locked me in a room while he attacked the domes? It happened. It's done." She stepped back as Kieran stood. "Fighting about who should have done what to protect me is pointless. I need to be able to protect myself. That's what I was trying to do before you and Jeremy started beating each other up."

Kieran's shoulders sagged. "I'm sorry."

"I'm so tired of *sorry*. Sorry doesn't bring people back to life or rebuild walls. I'm here because it's the only way I know how to survive, not because I want an apology."

"Then what can I do?" Kieran asked.

"Keep people alive and leave Jeremy alone. If Emanuel wants to hurt people, find a way to convince him to stop. Prove that you're worth being alive when other people aren't." Nola pressed her thumbs into her eyes. "I don't know what else to say."

"My dad will find a way to make more Graylock," Kieran said. "I'll do whatever it takes to help him."

"Who knows what else he can make of it?" Nola said. "Maybe he can find something in it to make ReVamp better for everyone. Maybe the next generation of vampires won't have to hide from the sun."

"What's the fun in being a creature of the night if you have to work during the day?" Raina shook her head. "I think vampires are perfect just the way we are. Also, I think I'll teach you to fight from now on. As entertaining as the boys' spat was, you still can't throw a decent punch."

Nola wavered between laughing and yelling at Raina for starting it all.

"First, I'll teach you to hit, then we'll move on to throwing knives." Raina's eyes sparkled with glee.

"I don't know if I'm a knife—"

The ground shook under Nola's feet.

The weapons hanging on the walls clanged as they bounced off the stone.

Nola squinted, trying to hear past the questioning voices of those around her. "What was that?"

"Nothing good." Raina ran for the tunnel that led toward the mountainside.

CHAPTER TWELVE

The ground rumbled again as Raina shoved open the giant metal doors.

"Was that an earthquake?" Kieran asked.

Nola's heart tumbled in her chest. She had read about earthquakes but had never felt one. The earth had spared their area from that curse, even as the sun's rays scorched and the rain hung heavy with poison.

"I don't think so." Raina ran down the tunnel, Nola and Kieran at her heels.

Nola's legs didn't mind the pace, nor did her lungs scream for air. Only when she looked at the tunnel walls sweeping past them did she realize how fast she was actually running. What felt like a gentle jog was really a full-blown sprint.

"I'm fast," Nola said, the words coming out easily. "I'm really fast."

"Welcome to the good life, Domer." Raina stopped, pressing her back to the wall as they reached the first window. The sun shone brightly through the gap, barely leaving enough space for Raina and Kieran to hide in the shadows. "Well shit."

"What?" Nola stepped in front of the other two, leaning toward the window.

Smoke billowed up from the city, rising in a thick shroud of black. Flames lapped at the buildings below, their brightness startling even in the morning sun.

"What happened?" Kieran said. "The riot fires have never been that big."

A light flashed in the city. Flames soared into the sky.

Tears streamed down Nola's face as the ground beneath her feet rumbled. "I don't understand."

"It's the Domers," Raina said. "They've finally had enough of their trashy neighbors."

"What?" Nola leaned out the window, desperate to see if any of the buildings in the city were still standing.

"The factories have shut down," Raina said. "The city is of no use to them. It's just a cesspit filled with people who want them dead. Why wouldn't they bomb the city?"

"Because there are children in the city," Nola said. "There are innocent people."

"Like Nettie?" Raina asked.

Nola froze.

"My baby sister is in that burning city, and the only crime she ever committed was being an alcoholic brat. I warned her for years, and she wouldn't listen. The house is gone, my sister is probably dead. And if not now, she sure as hell will be soon. Why? Because the domes want to live out the end of the world in peace, and the city is nothing more than a disease to be eradicated."

"We need to get out there and help people," Nola said. "Nettie could still be alive. There could be other survivors."

"You think the domes will let anyone out alive?" Raina said.

"We don't know what happened," Nola said, "but there are people out there who need our help."

"Or they're all already dead," Raina said.

"Nettie could be alive," Nola said. "We have to go find her."

"And do what?" Kieran watched the smoke rise. "We could rescue Raina's sister. But what about all the others you'd find. We couldn't bring them here. The domes would follow us back. They'd know where we are, and they'd attack. We don't have enough food to take in hundreds more people, and—"

"You sound like them," Nola said.

"I hate the domes, but they didn't get everything wrong." Pain pinched Kieran's brow. The bruises from the fight had already begun to fade.

"Kieran's right," Raina said. "Noah didn't load his ark with every living thing. He took what he could keep alive."

"You're supposed to be different." Nola shook her head. "Nightland is supposed to be different from the domes, to save everyone."

"If Emanuel could, he would," Kieran said. "That's the difference."

Another rumble shook the ground.

Nola spun back to the window. The flames that leapt into the sky were deep within the smoke, on the dome side of the city.

Will the glass even survive?

"We at least need to know what's going on," Nola said. "You say it's the domes, but it might not be. It could all be a huge accident. Or the werewolves destroying everything, or—"

"The domes," Rain cut across her. "No one else would be able to coordinate this."

"It could be someone we've never even heard about!" Nola shouted. "We need to go see."

"We'll talk to Emanuel," Raina said. "If he wants us to go, we can do it at nightfall."

"That's so long from now," Nola said. "How many more people could die in that time?"

"The Outer Guard could come slaughter us," Raina said. "They could come blast our tunnels and bury us alive. But it doesn't matter. We can't go until nightfall."

Kieran studied Raina's face.

"I'll go," Nola said. "I can run fast now."

"No," Kieran said.

"The sun would kill both of you, but I'll be fine," Nola said. "Even if I get burned, I can heal now."

"If you want to commit suicide, there are easier ways," Raina said.

"Jeremy will come with me," Nola said. "He won't let anything happen to me."

"Such confidence in lover boy," Raina said.

"We can't just sit in a tunnel while the city is blowing up," Nola said. "How far away is the city?"

"Thirteen miles," Kieran said.

"Okay." Nola nodded, the magnitude of the distance hurtling through her mind. "That's not too bad, right? I've had Graylock, I can do it."

"Absolutely not," Kieran said. "What if something happens to you? How would we find you? How are you going to find your way back?"

"He's right," Raina said. "You were knocked out for most of the trip. You'd get lost on the way back and die in the wild. *If* you made it to the city, and *if* you don't get attacked by any more rogue vampires. Or do you not remember the two who wanted to tear your throat out?"

"And Jeremy stopped them," Nola said. "What if the domes did attack the city? What if they're on their way here now?"

Kieran looked to Raina, who glared at Nola, her mouth twisted in a frown. "Fine, you get to go and play scout. You don't go into the city proper, and you get back here by nightfall. You drag lover boy out in the sun, see which group is running through the burning city in triumph and get out."

"We should ask Emanuel," Kieran said.

"Emanuel will agree with me," Raina said. "If she's going to go, she needs to go now."

"I'll get Jeremy." Nola took off back up the corridor, not waiting to hear the argument Kieran called after her.

She didn't know where his room might be, or if he even went back to where he had been sleeping.

The door to the sparring room burst open before Nola could reach for the handle.

"Nola!" Jeremy charged into the hall. "Are you okay?"

"The city is exploding. We have to go see what's happening." Nola took Jeremy's hand, dragging him back into the cavern.

"What?"

"The ground shaking—"

"Bombs are going off in the city?" Jeremy said.

"Yes." Nola stopped in front of the sparring vampires. "I need a backpack with water and food," she shouted over the fighting.

The sparrers turned toward her.

"Please."

No one moved.

"Raina said so."

The blond girl ran toward the back of the room, pulling a pack down from a shelf. "Ritchie, grab water and food."

The man she had pummeled less than half an hour before ran up the hall toward the main corridor.

"We don't keep those things in here," the blond said. "The water drinkers don't come to the sparring room very often."

The girl moved to hand the pack to Nola.

"I'll take it," Jeremy said. "You're strong, but you're still adjusting. We don't need anything throwing off your balance."

"Did you want any weapons?" the girl asked Nola as she handed the pack to Jeremy.

Nola's cheeks flushed. "Do you have any Guard guns? I know how to shoot those."

The girl nodded to a boy near her age. He opened the weapons locker and pulled out two belts with Guard guns and a slim silver box of darts.

"I'll take a knife, too," Jeremy said.

"Good," the girl said. "Keep to that if you can. Darts are worth more than blood."

"Thank you." The weight of the belt was no more than an egg in Nola's hands, but the reality of holding it took her breath away.

Where did they get this? Which guard's body did they take it from?

Jeremy strapped on his gun and tucked his knife into the side of his boot.

"I hope this is enough." The man who'd run down the tunnel returned, four bottles of water, five apples, and a loaf of seedy bread in his arms.

"It's plenty," Jeremy said. "We're not going far."

"We're going to the edge of the city." Nola strapped on the gun belt. Clasped as tight as it would go, the belt still hung low around her hips.

The man loaded the food into the bag.

"Is there anything else you need?" the girl asked.

"No," Nola said. "We'll tell Raina how much you helped."

Nola headed toward the door to the outer tunnel, Jeremy's boots thumping behind her.

"Are you sure about this?" Jeremy asked. "I can go on my own. I'll find out whatever we need to know and come right back."

"I'm going, Jeremy." Nola shoved the door open. "Either you can come with me and do the punching, or I can go by myself. It's up to you."

"No, it isn't." Jeremy stayed close on her heels. "If you're going, there's no choice in my coming along. You know that."

"You're right, I do." Nola ran down the tunnel. "Maybe next time don't argue with me."

"Trying to talk you out of doing dangerous things is as much a part of keeping you safe as punching duty."

Raina and Kieran came into view, both still pressed into the shadows, watching the window.

"Has anything new happened?" Nola asked. Her mind told her

she should be out of breath, panting from running down the hall, but the words came easily.

"A few more bangs," Raina said. "The domes are leveling everything."

Kieran glared at Jeremy. "Do the domes have the explosive power to pull that off?"

Another rumble shook the ground.

Jeremy peered out the window. "I wish I could say no."

A plume of fire danced in the air.

"I don't think they do," Jeremy said. "It was never in my training. I never saw a stash of explosives anywhere in the domes."

"Did you ever see the explosives they used on the bridge?" Nola asked.

"No," Jeremy said, "but we knew there was a plan. That's why the Dome Guard freaked out when Nightland broke in. They were never supposed to get across the river."

"But a plan to end the whole city?" Nola said. "How would they hide it, or pull it off?"

"Never underestimate what desperate people are capable of," Raina said. "How do you think Vamp happened?"

"Does Emanuel know what's going on?" Jeremy asked.

"I'm sure he does," Raina said. "He'll be hiding Eden by now."

"We need to go." Nola's fingers and toes tingled. "We need to know if anyone's coming after us."

After Eden.

"Jeremy can go alone," Kieran said.

"I've already tried that," Jeremy said.

"I'm going, so let's move." Nola stepped through the patch of sunshine.

"Don't play Pied Piper," Raina said. "If you let rats follow you back, you'll sink the ship. You save a pack of strays, you kill us all."

Dread settled into the pit of Nola's stomach.

"But if you find Nettie, bring her here," Raina said.

"I will." Nola nodded and started down the tunnel.

"Promise you'll take care of her." Kieran's words froze Nola in place.

"I will always take of her," Jeremy said. "Keep the door open for when we get back."

"We'll be waiting," Kieran said.

"Come on." Jeremy stepped up next to Nola. "If we're going to get back by dark, we're going to have to run."

"Let's run."

CHAPTER THIRTEEN

The gun thumped against Nola's hip, smacking her with every stride.

Will it leave a bruise? Or do I heal too quickly now?

The questions seemed absurd, but wondering about her hip kept away the thoughts of what the gun was meant to do.

"Do you really think it's the domes?" Jeremy said.

They passed another window in the long corridor. The city had disappeared behind the smoke.

"I don't know," Nola said. "Every time I think I know the line someone won't cross, they do it. Can the glass even withstand blasts like that so close by?"

"Yeah. The only way Nightland managed to blow a hole in the domes was by planting the charge on the glass itself. The domes were built to survive this sort of thing."

"Then it really could be them." Nola ran faster, her feet barely skimming the floor. She didn't bother slowing to look out the next window she tore past.

"Who's coming?" a voice shouted from around the bend.

"Nola and Jeremy," Nola called. "Raina's sent us to go and see what's happening in the city."

As they rounded the corner three vampires came into view.

Twin women, heads shaved and breasts barely covered by their artfully torn tops, flanked a gangly man with freckles coating his face.

"Raina wants you to go out there?" the man asked. "Is she trying to kill you?"

"That would be fun." The left twin smiled, baring her teeth.

"We're just trying to get information," Nola said. "We'll be right back."

"You'll burn without a sunny," the right twin said. "And no one gets to touch the sunny."

"What?" Nola shook her head. "We'll be fine in the sun, but you need to let us pass."

"Sun walkers who run like vampires." The freckled man tipped his head to the side. "What wonders have come to Nightland?"

"If you don't move right now, we're going to have to tell Raina you got in our way." Nola puffed her chest out and planted her hands on her hips.

The right twin and freckled man looked toward the left twin. The left twin's smile slipped away, her lips covering her teeth. Rolling her eyes, she stepped aside. The other two followed her lead, leaving a path down the middle of the hall.

"Thanks." Nola took off at a run, glancing behind to see the three glaring at her.

"Nola, watch out." Jeremy seized her arm.

Nola squeaked as Jeremy pulled her back from the ledge. Her lungs fought to reclaim the air fear had forced from them.

"Running faster means getting places faster." Amusement wrinkled the corners of Jeremy's eyes. "Super running lesson one: look where you're going."

"Lesson learned." Nola peeked over the edge. A patch of wilting grass waited ten feet below. "How do we get down?"

"Jump." Jeremy stepped up to the edge. "It's not too far. Hold your core for balance and don't forget to bend your knees."

He jumped off the edge like it was nothing more than the last step on a staircase, landing on the ground below with barely a sound.

"Right." Nola inched forward, placing her toes at the end of the moss-covered shelf.

"Don't worry, Nola," Jeremy said. "I'm right here. You'll be okay."

Nola pushed off the edge. Her heart vanished from her chest as reason told her pain awaited her on the ground.

She stumbled as she landed, tipping to the side and into Jeremy's arms.

"I've got you." He held her close to his chest. His heartbeat thundered next to Nola's ear.

"It didn't hurt." She stepped away from him. "I thought it would hurt."

"Your muscles are strong enough to cushion you now." Jeremy shrugged. "Don't try and push it too far, though. Jump from high enough, and even Graylock can't help you."

"You've never been scared of falling. You jumped out your bedroom window before you had Graylock." Tingles surged through Nola's chest at the memory of Jeremy jumping down to hold her, his face still creased from sleep.

"It was the fastest way down, and I wanted to get to you as quickly as I could," Jeremy said. "I won't lie, jumping out my window got a lot easier after I'd been given Graylock."

Nola stared into his eyes. Their color was the same brown it had always been, but lines of worry marked the corners, taking the place of the constant twinkle of joy that should have been there.

"We should go," Nola said. "It's going to be a long day."

"Yeah." Jeremy turned toward the city. "Run side-by-side, okay? I don't want you running into something I can't see, and I don't want you behind where I can't keep an eye on you."

"You don't trust me to take care of myself?" Nola tipped her head to the side. "I do know how to use the gun."

"Anytime I can't see you to know you're safe, it's like someone's lodged a stone in the back of my lungs. It hurts. And it steals my breath away. You've lived through things that would have killed some of the best Outer Guard." Jeremy took her hand in his. "Just stay where I can see you so I can breathe."

His fingers were warm and so familiar. It would be so easy to lace her fingers through his. They would run toward the flames together, their pulses keeping time.

"Okay." Nola pulled her hand away, adjusting her gun belt. "As long as it's not because you think I'm incompetent."

"I would never be that stupid."

Nola looked down the slope. The trees blocked the bottom of the mountain from view.

Down will be easier than up.

Rolling her shoulders back, Nola started to run.

The sloping ground made for longer strides, but her legs didn't tire. Keeping her gaze focused on the trees rushing past, she dodged between branches and ducked under low limbs.

Even running at top speed, she could see the details of the bark. Claw marks where an animal had mauled a tree, cracks where lightning had split a trunk open, decay where acid rain had worked its malice.

A waist-high rock protruded from the earth. Nola leapt onto the stone and down on the other side without breaking her stride.

"Now you're getting it." Jeremy beamed at her.

"This is amazing." The bottom of the mountain came into view. "No wonder they didn't want all the Domers to know what the Outer Guard were doing. Running this fast, it's like flying."

"It's pretty great," Jeremy said.

"But what?" Nola asked, hearing the hesitance in his voice. She looked over to him. "Ouch." They'd reached the bramble field, and the thorns tore at the back of her hand.

"Careful." Jeremy ran with his hands high over his head.

Nola did the same, feeling foolish as the brambles pulled at her pants like a thousand fingers searching for purchase.

"What's bad about being able to run this fast?" Nola asked.

"We're not wholly human anymore," Jeremy said. "We're different. If everyone took Graylock, there wouldn't be a next generation of humans."

She stumbled, her legs forgetting how to move for a moment. "There's T's baby. And Eden. We're not the end. We're not the last people who will live in this part of the world." Tears stung the corners of Nola's eyes. She pushed herself to run faster. "The fighting and fear are going to end. Somehow, someway. And children will be born, and this monstrous world will be nothing more than a scary story to them. I have to believe that, Jeremy."

The field ended, tossing them into the barren trees.

"If I don't believe there's going to be something good after all this, I don't know if I can keep going. I don't want to hurt people just to keep myself alive. But I can do it to protect T's baby. I can fight if it means keeping her baby safe."

"There will be something good after this." The gaps between the trees widened, and Jeremy moved to run right next to Nola. "I don't know what it's going to look like or who will be there to see it. But there will be people who do. And I'm going to do everything I can to make sure you're one of them."

"You have to be there too, Jeremy." Nola kept her eyes front, though she wanted more than anything to look at him. "I can't be the only superhero. I can't lose you."

His hand brushed the back of hers.

She didn't pull away.

Neither spoke as they ran past the body of the vampire who had attacked them such a short time ago. A dozen birds had found the corpse, taking advantage of the feast in mass.

The ground shook again, and again. They turned out onto a road whose surface had been cracked by weather and time.

Leaping over the potholes took more concentration than jumping over the roots of the trees.

"That one." Jeremy pointed between the trees to a two-story house whose red front door hung loose on its hinges. "That's where we spent the daylight. If something happens—"

"Nothing's going to happen."

"If it does, that's a safe place," Jeremy said. "Raina likes you enough, she might even come looking for you there."

"Looking for us," Nola said. "Say looking for *us*."

"She might come looking for *us*."

Nola hurtled over an eight-foot pothole.

"You can't go back to the domes. You know that, right?"

"They tried to kill you." Jeremy dodged around a rusted out, old car. Someone had driven sharp metal spikes into the sides. "I would never go back there. Not for anything."

"Then you have to promise you're coming back with me," Nola said.

"I promise."

A knot of fear Nola hadn't noticed melted, trickling down the back of her spine.

More houses lined the road as they neared the city.

The homes had all been built symmetrically. Fractured sidewalks met cracked driveways at regular intervals. These houses were so different from the crumbling stone apartment buildings in the city, Nola couldn't imagine what life in one of them must have been like. A little lawn all her own. A car to drive into the city. The peaceful life the domes strove to create. But this idyllic outside had failed.

What if the domes are failing right now? What if the domes are under attack as well?

Nola shoved the thought aside. There would be no way for her to cross the river to help, even if the domes didn't want her dead.

The road twisted around the bend, giving them a level view of the city.

Fire lapped at nearly every building in sight and lunged toward those that had been left unscathed by the flames.

Dense smoke settled on the wide track of road that led out of the city.

"We need to get off the road." Jeremy veered left into the thin line of dead trees that covered the fronts of the tumbled down houses.

"Why?" Nola followed him even as she asked the question.

"There are people on the road down there." Jeremy pointed to the wide highway at the edge of the city. "We don't want them to see us coming."

Nola squinted, trying to make out what Jeremy had seen. Dozens of tiny ant-like things moved around on the highway. As she watched, one ant charged another, sending the other dots scattering to the sides of the road.

Pain sliced through Nola's face as she tumbled backwards. The ground pummeled the air out of her lungs as she landed in the dirt.

"Nola." Jeremy knelt beside her.

"What happened?" Nola touched her cheek. Blood stained her fingers.

"You hit a branch." Jeremy pulled off the pack and took out a bottle of water. "Running into things hurts more when you're moving faster."

"I think there's a fight on the road."

Jeremy ripped off part of his sleeve. "Hold still."

Nola gritted her teeth as he poured water onto the gash.

"Sorry." He dabbed at the wound.

Each touch sent stars dancing in Nola's eyes.

"We have to get the tree bits out before you start to heal." Jeremy trickled more water onto her cheek. "Your body can work foreign objects out, but it hurts like hell."

"Thanks." Nola gasped as he pulled an inch-long splinter from her cheek.

"I think that's it." He trickled water onto her face again, peering into the wound. "You should be able to heal fine now."

"Is it really bad?" Nola cringed at her own whimper.

"You're still beautiful," Jeremy said, "and in an hour it'll be like it never happened at all."

He passed Nola the water bottle.

Nola took a long drink. The water trickled coolly down her throat, washing away the gritty dryness she hadn't noticed before.

Jeremy stood and looked out toward the road.

"Should we cut around the fight?" Nola asked.

Jeremy rubbed his hand over his face. "I say we head right toward it. That many people, someone is bound to know how all this started."

"Right." Nola sprang to her feet, a jolt of joy flipping in her stomach at the ease of her movement.

"We should go a little slower though." Jeremy pointed at the road. "People are starting to come up."

A group of ants had indeed moved beyond the fighting and up the road, all bunched together like they were afraid of being attacked at any moment.

Jeremy took a drink and tossed the bottle back in his pack.

"What if it was the domes?" Nola asked.

Jeremy started jogging, always choosing the path that allowed Nola room to run by his side.

"Jeremy?" Nola said when no answer had come for more than a minute.

"I just can't believe it could be them. That I served as a guard and never knew we had access to those sorts of weapons. That my father would give an order like that."

"He gave the order to kill me."

Jeremy flinched at her words.

"I thought that was the lowest," Jeremy said. "The worst thing my father could ever do, and to me it is."

"But if he ordered the destruction of an entire city—" Nola began.

"Then he had a lot further to fall than I ever imagined."

CHAPTER FOURTEEN

Nola peered out from her perch twelve feet up in a dying tree. Her arms didn't ache from the climb, and her fingers had no trouble clinging to the crumbling bark.

Four men and three women marched up the road. Two of the men supported a third between them. The fourth man leaned heavily on a woman's shoulder, while the other two women carried children in their arms. Soot stained all their faces. Blood and dirt marked their tattered clothes.

Nola shifted carefully on the branch that held her weight, ignoring the open air beneath her as she leaned toward Jeremy's ear.

"Where are they going?" she whispered.

Jeremy loosened his grip on the limb he dangled from, pressing his shoulder into Nola's. "I'm not sure they even know. They might not be running toward anything, just away from the city."

The urge to call out and stop the group, to tell them to hide in the house with the broken red door until she could lead them safely to Nightland, fought to burst from Nola's mouth.

The rats will sink the ship.

Anger tensed Nola's fingers. The bark cracked beneath her grasp.

"We should talk to them," Jeremy said, "find out what they know."

"We should help them," Nola said.

"We can't."

"We can go without eating for a day," Nola said. "We can at least give them the food."

Jeremy chewed his lips. "We keep an apple for each of us and give them one bottle of water."

"Deal." Nola let go of the tree branch and dropped to the ground, her legs holding steady as she landed.

The group looked toward her as Jeremy landed by her side.

From twenty feet away, the fleers looked even more pitiful than they had at a distance. Dark bags marred the skin under their eyes, and fatigue from years of survival marked their faces.

One of the children twisted to look at Nola. His tiny frame was no bigger than a toddler's, but his face made him appear at least seven.

"Stay away from us." One of the women pulled a rusted kitchen knife from her belt.

"We don't want to hurt you," Nola said. "We just want to know what happened in the city."

"How could you not know?" the man being supported by two others croaked.

"We were far away when the ground started shaking," Jeremy said. "We saw the explosions, but we don't know why they're happening."

"The fire came down from above," the youngest of the women said. "I was inside when the windows shattered."

"I heard buzzing overhead," one of the men said. "I looked up to see where it was coming from. A black and silver thing fell from the sky, then the street exploded."

"Do you know who was doing it?" Jeremy asked.

"I didn't bother trying to find out," the young woman said. "I saw Outer Guard though, swarms of them. They'll know."

"Do you think it was them?" Cold rushed through Nola's veins. "Do you think the domes did this?"

"Does it matter?" the wounded man asked.

"Where are you heading?" Jeremy asked.

"Away," one of the women said. "There's no place left to go but away."

"Here." Nola dug in Jeremy's backpack, pulling out the loaf of bread, apples, and a bottle of water. "It's not a lot. But maybe it can help until you find a place to rest."

The man who leaned heavily on the woman reached into his pocket, pulling out an old fashioned revolver, cocking it with a *click*.

"We're trying to give you something." Jeremy stepped sideways, planting himself in front of Nola. "Take the food and water and go."

"Your pack isn't empty," the man said. "You've got more in there and guns on your hips besides. Take off the belts and toss them over. Then drop the pack and food and walk away."

The man's hand didn't shake as he pointed the revolver at them. Nola wished it would. Wished he would show some hesitance at threatening their lives.

"Don't do this." Jeremy inched forward. "I'm asking you to walk away."

"We'll walk away once you've given us your supplies," the man said. "You can hand them over yourselves, or I can take them off your corpses. I don't care either way."

"I'm giving you one last chance to leave," Jeremy said.

"I'm the one with the gun drawn, and you're out of chances to listen."

Too many things happened at once.

Jeremy launched himself at the man, knocking his gun aside with one hand, and punching him in the face full force with the other. At the same moment, a *bang* shook Nola's lungs.

"Jeremy!" the scream tore from Nola's throat.

Her fingers fumbled as she pulled the gun from her belt, aiming it at the rest of the group, while Jeremy rolled off the man, revolver in hand.

Jeremy was on his feet a moment later. Blood dripped from his thigh, but his hands held steady as he pointed the revolver at the nearest man.

"We wanted to help you," Jeremy growled. "He shouldn't have had to die."

Nola glanced at the ground. The man who'd shot Jeremy lay still, his eyes wide, his neck twisted at an unnatural angle.

"You're going to run up the road," Jeremy said. "I'm going to give you one minute to get as far away from here as you can. If any of you are still in range after that minute, I shoot."

All six adults stared at him, a mix of horror and anger staining each of their faces.

"Go!"

At Jeremy's shout they ran. After ten seconds, the two supporting the injured man dropped him on the ground, picking up their pace to run in front of the women.

"No!" the man shouted. "Don't leave me, please!"

"Put the food back in the bag," Jeremy said.

"You're hurt." Nola tossed the supplies into the pack, pulling the top tightly shut. "You need help."

"I'll heal," Jeremy said.

Nola crouched by his leg. A hole dripped red on the front of his thigh. "There's no exit wound."

"The bullet's still in there."

"We have to get it out," Nola said. "How do I get it out?"

"You don't." Jeremy winced as he put his weight on his leg. "We have to keep moving."

"But it'll be awful." Nola glanced up the road.

The group had disappeared, leaving the injured man to crawl after them.

"You said healing with something stuck inside you is terrible. We have to get the bullet out."

"We need to move." Jeremy took Nola's elbow, leading her down the road at a run. "I don't know if any of the others have guns, and I really don't want to fight them. We need to get away from here."

They wove back into the trees at the side of the road.

Jeremy's gait had become uneven, but still his strides were longer than Nola's as they ran.

"Promise me you're going to be okay." Nola took Jeremy's hand.

"I promise," Jeremy said. "I can take a bullet in the leg."

He held her hand as they ran toward the highway.

Others passed on the main road, moving in the opposite direction. Toward the land of vampires they didn't know existed.

Some moved on their own, others in pairs or groups.

Nola cringed every time they were spotted. Her fingers itched to reach for her gun. Jeremy still held the revolver in his hand.

The revolver had scratches on the barrel and could hold only six bullets. A relic of another time.

"How do people still have guns like this?" Nola said. "Why didn't the Outer Guard take them all away years ago?"

"Officially, they did." Sweat trickled down Jeremy's brow. "But my dad runs into a few every year. Most of the time, the fools who held onto them for protection ended up dead."

"Like the man you killed," Nola said.

"I didn't want to kill him." Jeremy's face turned an unnaturally pale shade. "But he was pointing a gun at us. He would have hurt you."

"Jeremy." Nola tugged on his hand, stopping his limping run. "I don't blame you. We tried to help them, and he threatened to kill us. He had a gun."

Jeremy's eyes slipped down to the revolver in his grip.

Nola took his face in her hands. "Jeremy, he shot you. He could have killed you. If somebody had to die, I'm grateful it was him and not you."

Unshed tears pooled in Jeremy's eyes.

"You can't feel guilty for defending yourself. You kept us safe."

Jeremy nodded. In a moment, all trace of tears had vanished from his eyes, replaced with the determination of an Outer Guard.

"We've only got about a quarter mile until we reach the city limits," he said. "We need to see if whatever dropped the bombs is still in the air."

"Wolves don't have planes or helicopters." Nola took Jeremy's hand, leading him through the trees. "Neither do vampires. Something like that is beyond everyone's power. I don't even think the domes could pull that off."

"They couldn't." Jeremy tightened his grip on Nola's hand. "We've only got the skeleton helicopter, and that can barely lift two people."

They reached the edge of the woods.

The highway in front of them had been built for six cars to be able to travel down at once. The crumbling river of concrete separated the houses on the tree-lined street from the edge of the city.

Fires burned in the apartment buildings across the way. The tallest structure reached up seven stories, and flames danced high above the roof. Cutting between the buildings, a road four lanes wide with faded white dashes running in parallel lines provided the exit from the inferno of the city.

Evacuees funneled onto the path between the flames, all heading toward the six-lane road beyond.

Some stopped when they reached the old highway, turning back to gape in horror at the destruction of their city. Others, like the group they had met before, kept moving up between the tumbledown houses, heading into the wild unknown.

"There should be more coming out this way." Nola stepped out onto the wide road, craning her neck to see in either direction. The sweeping bend of the river that surrounded three-quarters of the city trundled downstream, caring nothing for the fires that torched the city its banks caressed.

"There's no other way out. The survivors need to come this way," Nola said. "Where is everyone else?"

"I don't know." Jeremy moved slowly across the road, weaving through the clumps of people who had stalled on the concrete.

"Mama!" a little girl cried, tugging on the sleeve of a weathered old man. "We have to go back and find mama!"

"She'll find us here." The old man didn't look away from the flames. "We have to wait here, and she'll come."

Nola looked back, willing herself to be strong enough to see the desperate child's eyes.

The girl had sores on her cheeks. Some illness had taken hold of her tiny body.

"We should have taken the food." A woman leaned against her husband's shoulder, tears coursing down her cheeks.

"What food did we have?" The husband pressed his lips to his wife's hair.

"We had six cans of beans, two cans of corn, meat stew," the woman said, ticking the list off on her fingers, "a filter for water, and one Nightland apple. We should have taken it all with us."

"The walls fell down, Dora." He held her tight. "We couldn't have gotten to the food even if we thought about it before we ran. All our supplies were destroyed before we left the doorstep."

"But I worked so hard—"

"We've got each other. Let's just be grateful for that."

Nola threaded her fingers through Jeremy's, pressing his palm close to hers.

"How could this happen?" A young man Nola's age turned his

back on the city to rage at the crowd. "Years of complacency and servitude. Working for the domes for money, for the Vampers to keep them from stealing the blood from our veins. Working for the wolves who promised us riches of food. But none have ever cared for us. None have ever wanted to keep the people who struggle everyday to have food and a place to sleep at night healthy. They only wanted us alive for their own benefit. This is what happens when our use is gone." The boy spread his arms wide. The flames of the city danced behind him like a cape of fire. "They've left us to burn with their trash. Our time of usefulness has ended. There is nothing left but fire."

The boy dropped his arms. He scanned the crowd, though what he was searching for Nola didn't know.

With a nod, he turned and ran back toward the city, not down the lane where the survivors drifted out, but straight toward the tallest building. With a *crash* the boy threw himself through the front door, disappearing into the flames.

CHAPTER FIFTEEN

"We have to help him!" Nola dove forward.

Jeremy caught her around the middle, lifting her off her feet. "There's nothing we can do, Nola. He's gone."

"But—"

"He's gone." He set her down, holding her tight.

Nola buried her face in Jeremy's chest. Tears streamed down her cheeks. A sob burst from her throat. "How?"

"I don't know." Jeremy pressed his lips to the top of her head. "But we're going to find out."

"We have to go in there." Her words came out between coughed sobs. "There have to be more people alive. We have to lead them to the way out."

"We can't," Jeremy whispered. "Going into the city is suicide."

"We can do it." Nola tipped her head up, looking into Jeremy's eyes. "How far away is Bellevue? That's where Raina's sister lives. If we can get to the street, we might be able to find her."

Jeremy shook his head, his arms tightening around Nola. "If I say *no*, will you listen to me?"

"No." Nola glanced toward the flames. The top floor of one of the buildings collapsed. Sparks shot into the air, cascading down in a rain of deadly fire. "I don't think I can live with myself if we don't try."

"If I say it's time to head back, you can't argue." Jeremy took Nola by the shoulders. "No matter how close we are, or who you want to help. If I say run, you run, and you don't stop till you're back in Nightland."

She nodded, wrapping her arms around Jeremy's waist and pressing her cheek to his chest for one more moment.

"How far to Bellevue?"

"Not far." He took Nola's hand, holding on tight as he started for the flames. "Only about ten blocks. We should be able to get in and out in a few minutes."

They reached the far side of the road. The heat from the flames pulsed against Nola's face. Her skin ached in protest, warning her to back away from the fire.

"Get out your gun." Jeremy let go of her hand. He pulled out his own guard weapon, keeping the revolver held tight in his other hand.

Nola pulled her gun free from her hip, checking the chamber and making sure the safety was off.

With a nod, Jeremy ran into the flames.

The heat lapped at them from all sides, but it was the sound Nola hadn't expected.

Screams echoed in the distance, far behind the *crackle* of flames. Before they had made it a block, a *crack* sounded behind them. A *screech* of crumpling metal sliced into Nola's ears as the building behind them collapsed.

Two figures ran out from the flames. A cape of fire trailed behind one. The flames consumed her body, a horrible wail carried through the blaze. Nola turned back to help.

"No!"

She froze at Jeremy's shout. The other figure stopped by the girl on fire.

For a moment, Nola thought the man would help. Stamp out the flames, find a way to heal her.

But the man looked up at the sky, his dark matted hair falling behind his shoulders. Black eyes glinted in the faint sun fighting to break through the smoke.

A groan poured from his mouth, but it was more than a sound. Blood followed the noise, trickling from his jaw. His shoulders shook as he dropped to his knees, raising his hands to shield his face.

He was too late.

Pink boils formed on his cheeks one moment only to burst the next, sending blood streaming down his face.

A scream echoed through the street. Nola knew the sound came from her throat, but she had no power to stop it.

The man clawed at his cheeks, as though to rip away the boils. His flesh tore free. Blood streamed freely down his chest. Blood leaked from his hands, dripping down his arms. He fell sideways, mauling his own face.

The girl coated in flames had long since stopped moving. But the man still writhed, tearing himself to pieces without seeming to know the damage he'd done. His nails found his neck, clawing a gap in his flesh. Blood spurted from the wound, coating the street in a rain of red.

He twitched on the ground, reaching to claw at his own legs. The plume of blood trickled out, and the man finally went still.

Nola's scream ended in a retch.

Jeremy's arm wrapped around her waist, guiding her forward though she could barely see through her tears.

"There's nothing we could have done for him." Pain crackled in Jeremy's voice. "He was dead the moment he went outside."

"They did it on purpose." Nola coughed, sucking more smoke into her lungs. "They're driving all the vampires out into the sun. They'll all end up like him."

"We can't do anything to help him." Jeremy pulled Nola to

run, pushing his weight unevenly off his wounded leg. "If we can get to Raina's sister, we might be able to save her, but there's nothing we can do to protect vampires from the sun."

"Get to Nettie." Nola wiped her tears away. "We're going to get to Nettie."

Jeremy let go of her, though he kept right by her side as they ran.

Smoke seared Nola's lungs. The foreign ache of it in her throat was enough to tell her she shouldn't be able to breathe. The smoke coating the street should have been enough to kill her. But the Graylock kept her lungs working, allowing her legs to pound against the cracked pavement with ease.

The farther into the city they ran, the more bodies they found of those who hadn't made it out of the flames in time. A scorched corpse lay in the middle of the street, splayed out as though they had jumped from a window, seeking a swifter death than fire would allow.

Another vampire, her black eyes the only part of her not disfigured by sores, stared up at the murderous sun even in death.

"I didn't know that was how it would look," Nola said.

"You shouldn't have to." Jeremy turned onto another road, down a row of houses that had yet to catch fire.

A group huddled in the middle of the street, staring at the inferno waiting on either end.

"You need to get out of here," Jeremy shouted to the group.

They all spun to face him.

"The Domers said they would come back." An older woman shook her head. "There was a whole swarm of them, and they said they would come back."

"They aren't coming. The fires are all over the city," Jeremy said. "Get to Main and then to the old highway."

"But the guards said to stay." A teenaged boy stepped in front of Jeremy, puffing his chest out though Jeremy towered five inches over him.

"The guards lied," Jeremy said. "You can stay here and burn or get out. If you wait much longer, there won't be any way out at all."

"Then where are you going?" a little girl asked.

"We're looking for a friend," Nola said. "But you've got to go."

"So do we." Jeremy walked past the cluster of people. "Go as fast as you can!" He called back as they ran down the road.

"Why wasn't that street touched?" Nola asked as they ran around the corner. "The fire should have spread that far by—"

"Nola!" Jeremy seized her arms, tossing her into the air.

Pain shot through her shoulder as she hit the ground ten feet behind Jeremy. In a second, he landed on top of her, covering her head with his chest.

"What?" Nola mumbled the question into Jeremy's shirt. "What!"

"Get up slowly, and stay behind me." He eased his weight off of her, kneeling in front of her until she scrambled to her feet.

"What was that about?" Nola rubbed her shoulder. The pain had already begun to fade.

"I know why this street isn't on fire."

Nola peered around Jeremy's shoulder. A silver and black metallic canister rested in the middle of the street. The pavement hadn't even cracked where the thing had landed.

"Is that a bomb?" Nola whispered, her voice stolen by the foolish feeling that speaking too loudly would cause an explosion.

"It's a fire pack." Jeremy took a step closer.

Nola grabbed his arm, pulling him back. "I don't know what a fire pack is, but please don't go any closer."

"It's pre-domes Incorporation tech. When blight started spreading, fire packs were used to purge the fields," Jeremy said. "Drop them from up high and torch everything below. A bang at the start of the cascade, then pure flames. The fire burns away whatever fungus or bacteria is killing the crops to keep it from spreading."

"Or wipes out the city to stop the people from spreading." A void enveloped Nola's chest. "The domes did this. Our home did this." She had no anger or tears. The void had swallowed the place where rage should have lived

"How did they get them?" Jeremy asked. "This many fire packs, there's no way they were stored in the domes, that's too dangerous. And how did they get them in the air?"

"We have to get to Nettie and get back to Nightland." Nola skirted around the fire pack, pressing her back to the buildings as she crept past.

"I don't understand." Jeremy followed Nola. "I just...how?"

"We're going to find out," Nola said, "but we've got to get Nettie."

They kept their backs to the buildings all the way around the corner until bricks blocked the fire pack from view.

"We're almost there." Jeremy took off down the street, glancing sideways to be sure Nola kept pace.

This street hadn't been burned either, but smoke hung heavy in the air.

Turning onto the next road, flames soared up in front of them. The stench of burning rubber singed Nola's nose. Fire had decimated the houses. The fronts of the buildings had caved in or toppled onto the street, leaving only burning skeletons of homes behind.

"We have to find another way." Nola gagged on the stench. "If we cut around—"

Jeremy took Nola's shoulders, turning her from the blaze. "There isn't another way, this is Bellevue."

"But..." Nola's protest faded as she looked back at the flames.

The twisted forms of melted lampposts dotted the street. The remains of stone stairs lead up to houses that no longer existed.

"No." Nola knew the word couldn't help but she shouted it anyway. "No, no, no!"

"We have to go."

She didn't fight him as he kept an arm behind her back, guiding her away from the blaze that was the end of Bellevue.

The fire pack still sat in the middle of the street.

How can a thing so small cause so much death?

No larger than her torso, the fire pack didn't look deadly at all. It could have been built to transport water or fuel for one of the domes' trucks.

But it's killed a city.

The group they had told to flee was gone.

"Do you think they made it?" Nola asked.

"We can hope." Jeremy didn't slow their pace, even as he favored his injured leg.

The smoke had thickened in the time they'd been in the city. Destruction that had been easy to see on the way in now hid beneath a sheet of smoke, as though the fire itself felt the disgrace of what it had done and wanted to hide the horror of its actions.

A boy lay in the middle of the street. Crumpled up like he'd been tossed aside. The slight rise and fall of his chest was the only thing that separated him from the other corpses they'd seen.

"He's breathing." Nola knelt next to the boy, rolling him onto his back.

It was the boy they'd spoken to only a few moments before. The one who truly believed the Domers would come for him.

"We can't leave him here." Nola slipped her arms under the boy. Gritting her teeth, she straightened her legs. She could feel the weight of him pulling her off center, but her arms didn't scream in protest.

"Give him to me." Jeremy reached for the boy.

"You're hurt. I can do it." Nola stepped back.

"He's bigger than you." Jeremy holstered his Guard gun, keeping the revolver in his other hand. "If we walk out of here with you carrying him, what will people think? They can't know we're different."

Nola helped Jeremy sling the boy over his shoulder.

"Are you sure you can do this?" Nola asked.

A gray tinge had taken over Jeremy's face, and sweat slicked his hair.

"We need to move."

Nola took the lead, weaving their way out to the alley between the walls of fire.

More buildings had collapsed, leaving flaming rubble coating the street.

Something that looked like a couch or a bed burned like a bonfire in the center of the path. Two charred corpses lay next to it.

With a wail and a *crack*, the façade of a storefront toppled onto the street in front of them.

"Is there another way out?" Nola shouted over the rumbling *crash* of an apartment building crumbling in on itself half a block behind them.

"No. Run, Nola."

"Not any faster than you." Nola pushed Jeremy in front of her, running right on his heels as he dodged between debris.

A glimmer of sunlight shone through the smoke ahead of them. A stretch of concrete filled with people.

"Almost there!" Nola shouted.

The top floor of a building sagged in on itself, showering Nola with sparks and catching the tip of her braid on fire. She patted the flames out with her palm, barely feeling the pain as her lungs seared, trying to find usable air within the shroud of smoke.

A *boom* sounded from far away, shaking the ground under her feet as they burst onto the highway.

"Out of the way!" Jeremy called.

He didn't stop until he reached the far side of the road.

"Help me," he said.

Nola grabbed the boy's shoulders, easing him carefully to the ground. The boy was still breathing, but his eyes stayed closed.

"Can you hear me?" Nola patted the boy's cheek.

"Nola." Jeremy grabbed her shoulder.

"He needs a doctor."

"Nola."

She looked up. Jeremy had his head down, his chin tucked to his chest.

Behind him, the street teemed with people. Some covered in soot. Some in the black uniforms of the Outer Guard.

CHAPTER SIXTEEN

"Oh no," Nola whispered.

Jeremy knelt in front of her, pulling the pack off his back. "Give me your gun belt."

Nola's fingers shook as she undid the clasp.

"Keep your head low." Jeremy slipped his own belt into the pack with Nola's and pocketed the revolver.

"Why are they all here?" Nola pulled her hair out of her braid, fluffing her unruly curls to hide her face. "How did they even get here?"

"No idea." Jeremy glanced back over his shoulder. "How many of them are there?"

Nola scanned the street through the curtain of her hair. "Two hundred, maybe three."

"Way too many." He shook his head. "A week ago, the domes were down to eighty-seven guards. Even with new people coming in we couldn't break one-fifty. The domes aren't built for it."

"Then who are they?"

"If you're in need of water, come over here," a voice shouted over the crowd. "Only one bottle per person. They are equipped with filters. Find a water source that isn't the river and the bottle will make the water pure enough to drink."

"They're giving out filters?" Nola stood, trusting in the crowd surging toward the voice to cover her.

"Why would they burn a city and help the survivors?" Jeremy said.

"It doesn't make sense."

"We need to get out of here," Jeremy said. "If they recognize us—"

"You mean you don't think your dad rescinded his kill order on me?" Nola knelt next to the boy. "We can't just leave him like this."

"His own people abandoned him in the middle of a burning street," Jeremy said. "We can't take him to Nightland, and I don't know the first thing about saving someone who's inhaled that much smoke."

"Please line up in an orderly fashion," a guard called from the center of the throng.

"What did they think was going to happen when they offered water to a few hundred desperate people?" Jeremy ran a hand over his face.

Guards surrounded the mass of outsiders. All had guns drawn.

"Remember to save these bottles," a guard instructed the crowd. "Keep them with you, and you'll be able to get more clean water."

"From where?" an angry voice shouted. "If we can't use the river, where should we go?"

"Where are we going to sleep and care for our wounded?"

"Why haven't you brought food!" a woman shoved a guard hard in the chest.

Two guards grabbed the woman, pinning her to the ground in an instant.

A *clap* like thunder sounded an instant later, pounding out from the center of the crowd.

Nola clamped her hands over her ears a moment too late. The sound throbbed through her brain, shaking away all thoughts but wanting the pounding to be gone.

The crowd scattered. Some falling to the ground and covering their heads, others stumbling away from the noise.

Only the Outer Guard in their heavy helmets didn't seem to mind the brain-shaking sound.

As the whooshing in Nola's brain settled, a man climbed up onto a set of crates. His limbs looked almost too long to be allowed, like the world had forgotten the difference between man and spider in his creation.

The man pulled off his helmet. His bald head glistened in the sun. "We have come out here in your time of need to offer aid. The domes are under no obligation to assist any of you."

Nola studied the man's face, wracking her brain to remember when she had seen him in the domes.

"We will leave in two minutes," the man continued. "If you would like a water bottle, calmly claim it now. Any unclaimed bottles will return with us to the domes." The man lifted his wrist, speaking into the cuff of his uniform.

The crowd surged forward, pushing each other out of the way to get to the center of the pack.

"We need one of those bottles," Jeremy said.

"I'll go." Nola stood.

"No, some of those guards could be from our domes."

"I have hair camouflage, you don't." Nola pulled more hair to cover her face, and ran toward the crowd.

She shoved her hands between two men, prying them apart, and slipped through the gap. Someone stomped on her foot. Stars danced in her eyes, but she pushed forward, shouldering past people until the crates came into view.

Rows of shining silver bottles sat in the crates. There were dozens of bottles in every crate and dozens of crates in the pile.

They were expecting more survivors.

Keeping her body smashed in the crowd, Nola reached her fingers out, barely managing to close them around a metal cylinder.

A fist swung for her face and nails scraped the back of her hand as she pulled her prize from the crate.

The punch connected with her forehead. She stumbled as arms wrapped around her chest, pinning her arms to her sides. She kicked back. A *crack* of breaking bones sounded the moment before the person holding her bellowed, their arms slipping away from her.

Cradling the bottle to her chest, Nola plowed her way through the crowd, back toward Jeremy.

The rumble of engines shook the air. The mob scattered, all moving in the same direction as Nola, knocking each other over in their haste to flee.

Heat licked the back of Nola's neck.

"Load them out!"

Nola glanced back at the shouted command. A helicopter large enough to hold all the crates landed on the street.

The guards pushed through the crowd, loading the crates onto the aircraft, then formed a line in front of it. All the guards' guns pointed at the crowd.

In less than a minute, the helicopter had been loaded and, with a whine of its engines, soared straight up into the air.

As soon as the helicopter had cleared, the guards turned, running down the highway toward the river beyond. Four dark boats had arrived on the riverbank, waiting to ferry the soldiers home.

An arm wrapped around Nola's waist. She jabbed her elbow backwards, catching the person who grabbed her in the ribs.

"Ouch." Jeremy coughed.

"Sorry." Nola stopped running, but Jeremy kept a hand on her back, pushing her forward. "I didn't know it was you."

"Then I'm glad you defended yourself."

Angry shouts took over the street as the sound of the helicopter faded.

A dozen brawls broke out in a matter of seconds as everyone fought for the bottles.

"How could they just leave like that?" The question barely made it through her gritted teeth. "They had to know everyone would fight to keep more bottles."

Footsteps pounded after them. Jeremy let go of Nola, catching their pursuer in the ribs with a punch.

"Run faster." Jeremy took Nola's hand.

"What about the boy?"

"He's still breathing and I moved him into the shade," Jeremy said. "There's nothing more we can do."

Nola bit the inside of her cheek, tasting her own blood.

Helping got Jeremy shot.

At least you didn't leave him to the flames.

They didn't bother sticking to the trees but sprinted up the center of the street.

Nola kept at Jeremy's side.

I could run faster.

But Jeremy's breathing came in rattling gasps, and his gait became more uneven every minute.

"We need to stop." Nola tugged on Jeremy's hand.

Jeremy didn't argue as Nola veered off the road and into the trees.

Others had followed their path, but none moved half so fast.

"We have a few minutes before they can catch up." She led him to a tree, pushing his shoulders to make him lean against the trunk.

"Give me the bottle." Jeremy coughed. He turned his head to the side and spat black into the brown grass.

"Are you okay?" Nola took his face in her hands.

"My body is purging, just give me the bottle."

Nola handed the silver bottle to Jeremy.

He didn't unscrew the top as she had expected, but flipped it over, examining the base.

"Do you want water?"

Jeremy ignored her. He dug his fingers into the seam at the bottom of the bottle.

"What are you doing?" Nola said.

He swayed as he reached down, pulling the knife from his boot.

"Jeremy."

"There has to be a reason." He dug the tip of the knife into the seam. With a *pop* the bottom came loose.

Another layer of metal waited beneath, as smooth and shining as the outside. A blue triangle run through with tiny lines had been stuck to the very bottom.

Jeremy pulled the triangle loose and held it up to the sunlight.

"What is it?" Nola whispered.

"It's a beacon. They're in the wrist cuffs the Outer Guard wear. It's how the domes track guards when they're out in the city."

"And they've planted them on all the survivors." Nola took the water bottle, unscrewing the top before looking back to Jeremy. "Can I drink it?"

Jeremy nodded. "No use in tracking dead people."

Nola took a long drink of the cool water, letting it dampen the fear rising in her chest.

"The domes destroyed the city and gave trackers to the ones who made it out alive." Her mouth went dry. She took another long drink. "They're trying to find Nightland. The guards are banking on some of the survivors making it to the vampires, and Emanuel taking them in."

"He won't." Jeremy pushed himself away from the tree. "No one will find Nightland. We'll warn Emanuel. We won't let the guards find them." A groan of pain slipped from him as he put weight on his leg.

"We have to get the bullet out." Nola pushed him back to the tree.

"It's already working its way out." Jeremy pushed himself up again, not seeming to notice Nola's hands on his chest.

"What do you mean working its way out?"

"It's like getting shot, but really slowly, and in reverse." His mouth narrowed into a thin line, and pink splotches blossomed on his forehead.

"We have to get it out." Nola grabbed his arm, trying to pull him back, but he kept walking toward the road, dragging her along behind him.

"We have to get back and tell Emanuel what the domes have done." Jeremy spoke through clenched teeth. "We have to warn them not to take anyone in, we need to tell Raina we couldn't find her sister, and I need to get you safely into those caves before the desperate people who just lost their homes catch up to us. I'm not sure if you noticed, but I'm not in fighting shape right now. Our best bet is to keep ahead of the crowds, so we have to move."

He stared into Nola's eyes, fierce determination pushing past his pain.

"Okay." She laced her fingers through his. "We'll get back to the caves."

Jeremy dropped the blue triangle onto the ground and downed the rest of the water.

Nola let him set the pace back to the road, keeping right by his side and scanning the tress for more guards with gifts or men with revolvers.

Jeremy tossed the bottle back onto the road.

No point in risking more trackers.

Nola opened her mouth to say something, anything to distract him from his pain. She couldn't think of any words.

She glanced behind.

A group of survivors had reached the spot on the hill where

they'd stopped. Jeremy had been right to make them keep moving.

The caved in houses gaped at them as they passed, as though judging the world that had let safety deteriorate. The run down old buildings were the closest things to home the survivors would be able to find.

They passed the house with the red front door.

"They're going to fight over the houses aren't they?" Nola asked. "Even if they can find water and food, they'll start fighting each other."

"Or the vampires and werewolves will come for them when the sun goes down. There might have been some hiding deep enough down that they survived. If they did, they'll come out when the sun sets, furious and ready for a feast."

The incline of the road steepened as they neared the trees. Jeremy glanced behind then pushed himself to run faster.

Nola looked back. The groups behind them were nearly out of sight. A little faster and no one would be able to see where the two first up the hill had disappeared.

They stayed silent as they ran through the trees. The only sounds the thumping of their feet and the branches clawing at their clothes.

The sun had begun to sink when they reached the field of brambles.

How many sunsets since I've slept?

A wave of unbearable fatigue swept through Nola, adding a hundred pounds to each of her limbs and sand to her eyes. But Jeremy kept running.

All the color had faded from his face. Pink and gray had disappeared, replaced by sickly white.

"Almost there." Nola lifted her arms over her head, away from the thorns that clawed at her legs. "We're almost there, and then Dr. Wynne will get the bullet out. We'll sleep when we get there, and then you'll feel better."

"Will you stay with me?" Jeremy's forehead furrowed with pain. "You could have burned to death today, can you just stay where I can see you're safe?"

Nola coughed a laugh. "I'm fine, Jeremy."

"It's hard to remember when I wake up."

They reached the stripped trees, and the path grew steeper still. Nola wrapped her arm around Jeremy's waist, helping to propel him up the mountain.

"I've almost lost you so many times," Jeremy said. "When I wake up, it's hard to believe you still being here isn't just a dream. I always have this second of panic. I have to go through all of it, just to make sure I haven't lied to myself. That you really are alive. I hate that second. It's worse than any bullet."

Tears stung the corners of her eyes. "I'll stay where you can see me. You won't have to panic. I'll be right there with you."

"Thank you."

Jeremy led them up the mountain, though Nola didn't know how he could see the path through the sweat that dripped into his half-closed eyes.

"Here," he wheezed as the sun kissed the tops of the mountains.

Nola searched the slopes around them. The moss-covered ledge peered out overhead.

What had seemed like an impossible leap a short time ago looked easy now.

"I'll boost you up." Nola made a step with her hands.

"You just go." Jeremy shook his head, stumbling at the movement. "I'll be fine."

"You first then." Nola took a step back. "I'm not jumping up there without you."

Jeremy turned in a slow circle, scanning the trees around them. He looked back at the ledge, squaring his shoulders, and pushed off.

A moan escaped him as his fingers caught the ledge.

"Let me help you." Nola reached for his legs, but he had already begun to pull himself up.

His arms shook, and his breath hissed through his teeth.

Nola covered her mouth with her hand, biting back the urge to shout for help from above. Her palm smelled like smoke.

With a feeble kick, Jeremy's legs disappeared from view.

"Come on up." His voice sounded like he'd been sick for a week and the dome doctors had decided to ignore him.

Nola bent her knees and aimed her weight for the ledge. Her palms landed on the soft moss. Pushing with her arms, she leveraged her weight up and over the edge. She stumbled on the stone ledge, but stayed on her feet.

Jeremy sat, propped up against the tunnel wall. "You're a pretty quick study."

CHAPTER SEVENTEEN

"Nola!" Kieran's voice carried out of the tunnel. "Nola, are you hurt?"

"I'm fine." Nola looped an arm around Jeremy's waist, hoisting him to his feet. "Jeremy's hurt. He's got a bullet stuck in his leg."

"Shit." Footsteps ran up the tunnel. Kieran stopped in the shadows ten feet down the entrance. "Can you get him this far?"

"We've gotten all the way up from the city," Jeremy wheezed. "We can make it to Emanuel."

Jeremy leaned on Nola's shoulder. The weight felt heavier than it should have. Whether from fatigue or knowledge of the horrible pain that weakened him, Nola didn't know.

"Lover boy got a bullet in the leg and you didn't pull it out?" Raina appeared by Kieran's side.

"Didn't have time," Jeremy said. "It's been a bad day out there."

One shuffling step at a time, they reached the shadows.

"Let me see it." Kieran knelt by Jeremy's leg.

"I'll go to your father," Jeremy said.

"How long has it been in there?" Kieran asked.

"Too long for a few more minutes to make a difference," Jeremy said.

"What's going on in the city?" Raina asked.

"I..." Nola searched for the words.

"There is no more city," Jeremy said. "We tried to find your sister. Bellevue is gone."

Raina nodded, her face betraying no grief at hearing of her sister's end. "We need to get you to Emanuel."

Jeremy limped a step forward.

Kieran raised a hand to stop Jeremy. "I'll carry you. It'll be faster."

"No chance in hell," Jeremy coughed.

"*I'll* carry you." Raina walked up to Jeremy and scooped him over her shoulder. "Don't argue and don't kick. I'm in a bad mood."

Jeremy mumbled a response as Raina ran down the tunnel.

Say that you ran into the fire to look for Nettie. Say you tried but the flames were stronger. Tell them about the guards and the fire packs. Tell them about the beacons in the water bottles.

Nola could only form thoughts as they ran up the tunnel. No speech would come.

Raina slowed at each of the windows, carefully keeping her skin in the shadows.

The sunset tinted the sky brilliant, lively colors, filled with the promise of a brand new tomorrow. But the smoke of the city stained the horizon, tainting its grandeur.

Kieran ran in front of Raina, wrenching open the metal door to the sparring room.

Every match stopped as Raina entered the room. A chorus of shouted questions echoed off the walls.

"Are they coming for us?"

"What have the Domers done?"

"Were the wolves finally slaughtered?"

"We have to talk to Emanuel first." Raina didn't slow her pace as she shouted over the crowd. "Once we've talked to Emanuel, he'll let everyone know what's going on."

"Is the sun runner dying?"

Nola spun toward the voice.

The blond girl stared back at her.

"He's not dying," Nola growled. "He's going to be just fine."

"Good." The blond winked.

Nola curled her hands into fists as she chased after Raina.

"He shouldn't have left a bullet in this long," Kieran said.

A group of six women carrying mismatched baskets plastered themselves to the wall as Raina ran past. One dropped her load, sending clean sheets spilling onto the floor.

"*He* can hear you," Jeremy said, "and *he* didn't really have many options."

Kieran reached the double door to Emanuel's library first. He only managed to knock once before Raina shoved him aside and flung the door open.

"Raina!" a little girl squeaked, running toward their group.

Eden.

Nola's heart melted at the sight of the child.

Black curls surrounded her round, rosy cheeks. Her big, dark eyes sparkled as she reached up for Raina.

"Go get your father and Dr. Wynne," Raina said.

A flicker of hurt wrinkled the child's forehead before she ran for the library door, calling, "Daddy! Doctor!"

"What's happened to Jeremy?" Julian stepped away from the bookshelf, a mug clasped in his hands.

"Bullet," Nola said.

Raina eased Jeremy off her shoulder and laid him on the floor. "Take off your pants like a good boy."

Jeremy shook his head.

"The world is ending," Raina said. "It's not like we've got pants to spare."

Planting a foot on Jeremy's chest, Raina undid his pants. "Do you want the honors, or should I?" Raina winked at Nola.

Heat flashed in Nola's cheeks.

"Oh for heaven's sake." Julian knelt by Jeremy's feet and pulled his pants down in one swift tug.

"I didn't know your talents in this field were quite so impressive," Raina said.

"Years of practice." Julian untied Jeremy's boots.

Instinct told Nola to help him, but she couldn't move. Couldn't think beyond anything but Jeremy's bare legs.

He still wore his dome-issued briefs, but they only reached halfway down his thigh. Nothing covered the wound on his leg.

Red streaks spread out like a spider's web over his thigh, surrounding a bump that moved with each of Jeremy's heartbeats, pulsing up as though fighting to break free.

"We have to get that out of him." Nola shook her head. Her body didn't know what else to do. "It's infected."

"If Graylock is as good as it's supposed to be, he'll be fine," Kieran said.

Emanuel came through the back door, a confused Dr. Wynne on his heels.

"Nola, what's happened?"

"Jeremy needs help." Nola pointed a shaking finger at Jeremy's leg.

"What did the two of you get into?" Dr. Wynne knelt by Jeremy.

"He got shot, and the bullet—"

"Leaving those sorts of things in there really isn't a good idea, you know." Dr. Wynne fished in his pockets, first pulling out a spray bottle, then a metal case.

"I tried to convince him to let me try and get it out, but he didn't think we had time."

Dr. Wynne popped open the metal case. Three scalpels waited inside.

"What did you find out there, Nola?" Emanuel asked.

"The domes dropped fire packs on the city," Nola said. "They destroyed the whole thing. I don't think there will be a building left standing when the fires go out."

The doctor sprayed foam onto the pulsing lump on Jeremy's leg.

"Why?" Julian asked. "That many fire packs so close to the domes, it seems like an unreasonable risk. With the bridge destroyed, the city is hardly a threat."

"They think it is," Nola said. "There were Outer Guard in the city, and not just from the domes here."

"Salinger," Jeremy groaned. "It was Salinger."

"What?" Nola knelt beside him, taking his hand.

His eyes flickered open. "The man who spoke. I couldn't remember why I recognized him. Salinger."

"This might sting." The doctor sliced into Jeremy's thigh.

Jeremy clamped his mouth shut, swallowing his shout as white leaked from the wound.

"You're okay." Nola squeezed his hand. "This'll make it better. Soon it'll feel better."

"Might need to go a bit deeper." Dr. Wynne wrinkled his brow.

"Who's Salinger?" Kieran asked.

"He's from the Incorporation." Julian pinched the bridge of his nose. "An evil man whom I had hoped to never hear of again."

"The Incorporation's here?" Raina tipped her head, her mouth pinched as though trying to reason through why a joke might be funny.

"Just a bit deeper and I should have it." Dr. Wynne pressed the scalpel into Jeremy's leg again.

Jeremy shut his eyes. A groan rumbled in his chest.

Blood trickled from the wound.

"You're okay." Nola pressed her forehead to his. "Just breathe, you're okay."

"The domes we have dealt with for so long are but one of many," Julian said. "They were all incorporated under the same project. All meant to trade people, supplies, and knowledge as the world dwindled to nothing. And, of course, all spread out in an appropriate manner for repopulating the world once the planet has found a path back to sustainability."

"Salinger is from another set of domes?" Emanuel asked.

"Yes," Julian said, "but the more worrisome and deadly part of the equation is his place as head of the guards. All of the guards, in all of the domes."

"Just another moment." Dr. Wynne tipped the scalpel into the wound.

"Shh," Nola hushed. "You're okay."

"Why would the head of all the guards be here?" Raina asked. "They blocked themselves off. The fight is over."

"They want Nightland," Nola said.

"Gah!" Jeremy shouted as Dr. Wynne pulled the bullet free.

"There you are." Dr. Wynne held the hunk of metal up to the light. "Such a tiny thing to cause so much pain. I would offer to stitch you up, but a nice lie down and you'll be fine."

"What do you mean *they want Nightland*?" Emanuel pressed.

"Salinger wasn't there shooting people," Nola said. "They were waiting for survivors and giving out water bottles complete with filters that will make anything but the river water drinkable."

Julian whistled. "That is a gift I had never thought the domes would consider giving."

"They had beacons hidden in the bottoms," Nola said. "They're tracking where all the bottles go. They destroyed the city and are making the survivors lead them anywhere people might be hiding and surviving. People like Nightland."

"Damn," Julian whispered.

"Raina," Emanuel said, "double the guards at every entrance. There is to be absolutely no one entering or leaving Nightland. If anyone has any qualms with my ruling, send them directly to me."

"Yes, Emanuel." With a nod, Raina ran out the door.

"Julian, check the gardening tiers and the air shafts. Make sure we can't be seen from below."

"Or above." Nola looked to Kieran. "They had a big helicopter, big enough to fly over the mountain. If they see the garden, they'll know we're here."

Kieran's black eyes widened in fear. "We have to take all the sun disks down. We can pull brush to cover the tiers."

"Do it."

Kieran and Julian were out the door before Emanuel could speak again.

"Is there anything else we need to know?" Emanuel stood with his hands behind his back, his shoulders relaxed even as terror filled those around him.

"I don't think so. It's going to be bad out there. None of the survivors have anything, and..."

"And you can't believe the domes would do such a thing?" Dr. Wynne patted Nola's shoulder, leaving behind smudges of Jeremy's blood. "I *can* believe it. Each dome is a part of a greater plan. Our dome has been struggling with the city for some time. If the Incorporation had to become involved, there is nothing they would consider unreasonable for the protection of the domes."

"So they fly in on their fancy helicopter and fix the problem? Captain Ridgeway couldn't control the city so just kill everyone to clean up the mess?" Nola looked from Emanuel to Dr. Wynne, waiting for one of them to tell her how wrong she was.

"The Incorporation believe their mission is the only hope for the world," Dr. Wynne said, "and only those chosen to save the world can truly matter. Everyone else is already doomed and none of their concern."

"The domes are monsters." Nola's hands shook.

Jeremy pressed them to his chest, his eyes still closed.

"I'm afraid so." Dr. Wynne stood. "I saw it many years ago. A simple vaccine could have stopped so much illness in the city. I was reprimanded for wasting my time in saving those outside the glass. For years I sat in the sterile domes, pretending the children out in the world who were suffering and dying had nothing to do with me. But they did. I failed to serve them when I had the knowledge and resources. I let them die because I didn't know their names. When I couldn't stand it any longer and found a way to help the outsiders, the domes found out and left me and my son out to die. They are kind only to those they need and killers to everyone else. I can think of no better definition of *monster*."

"You hated us for breaking into the domes." Emanuel knelt in front of Nola.

Tears streamed down her face as she looked into his black eyes.

"To the Nola Kent who lived safely in the domes, we were monsters seeking destruction," Emanuel said. "To the Nola Kent I see now, the monsters surrounded her the whole time. I led freedom fighters into the demons' lair to protect children the domes would gladly burn."

Nola coughed a sob.

"I ask your forgiveness for the blood we've shed to build our home," Emanuel said. "The path to salvation has led us through many dark and terrible places. I never wanted to fight the monsters. I only wanted my child to survive."

"Am I a monster for living with them for so long?" Nola said.

"Not at all." Dr. Wynne packed away his scalpels. "If that were true, Kieran and I would be monsters as well. And I hope you don't think that of me."

"No," Nola said. "You're a hero and a healer. I just..."

Jeremy lifted Nola's hand, pressing it to his cheek.

"I thought I knew which direction was up," Nola said. "And I don't know what to do now that I can't even pretend I wasn't wrong."

"You forgive yourself," Emanuel said. "You forgive others, and you work."

"The work is the part that helps most," Dr. Wynne said.

Jeremy's hand slipped from Nola's, falling gently to the floor.

"We need to get him someplace to sleep," Nola said.

"His room is right down the hall." Emanuel lifted Jeremy, carrying him like a small child.

"What happens if they find us here?" Nola followed Emanuel into the hall.

"They will attack us," Emanuel said.

"Can the fire packs get down this far?" Nola asked.

"If they come for my family, they will bring far worse than fire packs." They stopped three doors away from the library. "If you would?"

Nola twisted the nob. The door opened without a *creak*.

A single bed waited along with a desk and a chair.

"Is this where he's been sleeping?" Nola pulled back the sheets on the bed.

"It seemed right." Emanuel laid Jeremy carefully down.

"To keep him so close to you and Eden?" Nola said. "Not that he would ever hurt you."

"Keep your friends close and your enemies closer," Emanuel said. "My grandmother always used to say that."

Emanuel stepped around her to the open door.

"Do you think he's your enemy?" Nola asked before the door could shut.

"No." A weary smile curved Emanuel's lips. "But shattered hearts are the enemies of all men, and that boy has been broken. I can only hope that somehow my friend's heart will be pieced back together."

The door closed with a *click*. The tiny noise seemed louder than the *bang* of the revolver.

Every muscle in Nola's body screamed for sleep. Her legs longed to collapse.

Jeremy lay in the bed, his chest gently rising and falling. Color had already begun returning to his face.

Tears slipped down Nola's cheeks. She didn't bother drying them, or untying her shoes before wriggling her feet free.

Jeremy's arm splayed out to the side, as though even in painful sleep he'd remembered to leave a place for her.

She curled up next to him, tucking her head onto his shoulder. His chest rose and fell with each breath. Another inhale, another victory. Another moment the end of the world hadn't stolen from them.

Sleep came for her before she could wonder how close the end might be.

CHAPTER EIGHTEEN

Jeremy's arm moved, pulling Nola out of sleep.

"Don't," Nola mumbled, burying her face in his chest. "Don't move."

Beneath the stench of smoke, he still smelled like him. Like fresh earth.

I hope that smell never goes away.

"You don't want me to move?" His words rumbled in his chest.

"No." Nola wrapped her arm over his stomach, pulling herself closer to him. "If you move, then I have to open my eyes."

"You don't want to?"

Nola could hear Jeremy's smile shaping his words.

"No, I don't," she said.

He leaned his cheek against her hair.

They lay silently for a long moment. Footsteps passed in the hall. Life in Nightland continued without their aid.

"Does your leg still hurt?" Nola asked.

"It feels fine. I'll stretch it out a bit and be good as new."

"I should let you get up then."

Jeremy held her tight. "You shouldn't."

A child ran past in the hall, laughing about something.

"If I open my eyes, then we have to go out there." A tear leaked down Nola's cheek. Her hands started to shake. She balled them into fists, gripping the front of his shirt. "If we go out there, then I'll know yesterday wasn't just a nightmare. And the domes murdered people, and Nightland is in hiding, and I don't know if I can deal with all of that."

He pressed his lips to the top of her head. "I wish I could tell you it was all a bad dream."

"You promised not to lie to me again," Nola said.

"I know."

Nola wiggled up higher on the bed, pressing her forehead to Jeremy's cheek.

"Remember before all of this started, when the zombie woman made it to the outside of the domes?"

"Yeah."

"I thought she was terrifying," Nola whispered. "I thought the kids in the food lines on Charity Day were the saddest thing I would ever see. I was so stupid."

"Not stupid. You were never stupid. Maybe a little naïve, but we were kids. We weren't supposed to know how messed up everything is."

"It wasn't that long ago, you know?"

"A lot's happened."

"Yeah."

They lay still for a long while. Nola's breaths matched Jeremy's, their chests rising and falling in time.

"Promise me we'll both make it out of this?" Nola whispered. "You and me together."

"Nola..."

"You've never broken a promise to me." She found Jeremy's hand, lacing her fingers through his. "So promise we're going to get through this."

"I would never let anything happen to you." Jeremy's lips brushed her cheek as he spoke.

Nola opened her eyes, turning so her face was a breath from his.

"I don't need you to protect me. I don't need you to fight my battles or pretend everything is okay just to make me feel safe."

"I know. I just"—a shudder shook his shoulders—"the idea of anything happening to you, it kills me."

Nola leaned in, brushing her lips against his. A tingle squirmed at the bottom of her toes.

"I love you." She rested her forehead on his. "I can fight for myself, but I need as many things worth fighting for as I can get. I need to know at the end of all this, you'll be by my side."

"I promise you, Magnolia Kent, when all this is over, I'll be with you." He brushed the curls from her face. "As long as you let me, I'll be by your side."

Nola pressed her lips to his, letting the warmth of their kiss flood her chest, sweeping away all thought of fear and worry.

Jeremy wrapped his arm around Nola's waist, pulling her closer.

She separated her lips, deepening their kiss. Her pulse thundered in her ears, but beyond the steady thumping off her own heart, she could hear Jeremy's blood racing through his veins, his pulse keeping time with hers.

His fingers found the skin at her hip. Heat throbbed from the trail his fingers traced up her spine.

Nola found the bottom of his shirt. His hands joined hers as she pulled it up, snaking the fabric over his head.

No scars marked his chest. All of the blood and pain had left his skin unharmed.

She pressed her lips to his chest. Never had she been so grateful for the simple sound of a beating heart.

He took her face in his hands, kissing her cheeks, her lips, trailing his kisses down her neck.

She shifted her weight, twisting to sit.

He lay on the bed beneath her. His short hair tousled from sleep, the lines of worry fading from around his eyes.

His hands slid up her sides as she pulled off her shirt.

She lay down, pressing her chest to his.

"Nola." Her name fell from his lips as she kissed him.

Their limbs twined together as they searched for every inch of flesh they could share.

All thought of where she ended and he began disappeared. All fear of what lay beyond the moment vanished.

There was nothing left in the world but them and the darkness.

CHAPTER NINETEEN

The thick smell of fertilizer filled the air. Even with the cloth tied over her face, the inside of Nola's nose itched from the scent. Footsteps echoed dully in the cavern, and water trickled down the back wall.

While no glamour could be found working in the mushroom field, Nola welcomed the peace.

Kieran had banned visitors from entering the lowest cave in Nightland without his permission, and his consent was not easily given.

Nola pulled a glass vial from her bag. Carefully, she dug the vessel into the dirt. Fumbling in her thick gloves, she worked the stopper into the vial. She plucked the mushroom nearest where she had taken the sample, and wrapped the two in a rag before placing them in her bag.

The task she'd been assigned was simple enough. Find the best fertilizer for the different growing conditions in the mushroom field.

She chuckled to herself at the absurdity of calling this place a field. Buried deep in the mountain, the mushrooms were grown in a cavern the architects had barely altered. Most of the field consisted of random patches of growth rather than rows of crops to be harvested.

Lights hung from the ceiling at odd intervals, doing little more than casting strange shadows. Nola didn't mind. As long as a trace of light existed, Graylock gave her the power to see. Only absolute darkness could blind her now.

Humming faintly to herself, Nola wandered down the twisting paths of the cavern. Tucked up under a ledge, a patch of mushrooms fed off the water dripping from a crack in the wall. She scraped a bit of soil away from the base and plucked a mushroom sample as well.

None of the food eaters in Nightland relished the thought of living off of mushrooms for the cold months. In the week since Nola had started working in the caves, some had even gone so far as to question if she really needed to work on growing *more* mushrooms.

They'll be grateful if the other supplies begin to run out.

If they come for us.

Nola shivered, the chill of the cavern suddenly biting her to the bone.

She worked her way farther down the path, squeezing between a set of stalagmites to reach a growth of mushrooms that clung to the wall.

There had been no news from the city in more than a week. Raina said the smoke had stopped rising, and the stench had finally left the air. Emanuel had put her in charge of the ones set in the windows to watch the woods.

Nola would never dare say it, but she knew Raina spent her time scanning the outside world through that open window, searching for her sister.

Nola clasped her hands together, waiting for their shaking to stop before she pulled another glass vial from her bag.

A few lost survivors had been spotted at the base of the mountains wandering aimlessly. Searching for the safety and supplies they couldn't know were so close by.

She pulled down a half-moon shaped mushroom from the wall and tucked the sample safely in her bag.

The helicopter hadn't been spotted, but the tiered garden on top of the mountain still stayed covered. Only vampires were allowed out at night to silently tend the crops in the darkness.

At least the growing season is over anyway. And there was time to protect the animals. And the domes haven't dropped fire on us.

Slipping back through the stalagmites, Nola moved on to the main chamber of the cavern, to the part of the mushroom farm constructed by Kieran. The ceiling towered fifty feet overhead, and the space reached two hundred yards before meeting a pool. Then who knew how much farther until it ended?

We should try and farm fish in the water. There has to be a species that would thrive.

The domes hadn't trained her in animal husbandry. Just like they hadn't trained her in fighting or first aid.

She shook off the flare of anger that bubbled in her chest.

"Do the work you know how to do, Nola."

Each of the plots had been built of heavy-tarred wood filled with soil and fertilizer. Mushrooms blossomed at odd angles, thriving in the damp air. She worked quickly, moving from bed to bed, taking the samples that would help them expand the mushroom farm.

What Kieran had built didn't take up even a tenth of the space, and there was more room between beds than necessary. If they figured out the most efficient soil, condensed the beds, and spread out the operation...

Kieran and I will be the most hated people in Nightland.

Nola laughed. The sound bounced around the cavern.

A face appeared from behind a stalactite. A scowling, weathered old man with black eyes.

"Sorry," Nola whispered, knowing the man would easily hear her even at a distance.

Carefully dusting off her gloves, she tucked them into her bag with the last of the samples.

The face disappeared.

Nola rolled her eyes and headed for the pool. She could understand the man's love of the quiet. The peace was part of what made working in the mushroom fields worthwhile.

The tension above held nearly as strong a scent as the fertilizer in the cavern. Hardly anyone ever chose to venture outside Nightland, but now that it had been banned, stir crazy vampires roamed the halls. Between all the brawls that had broken out and the constant threat of hundreds of guards swooping in on them, the cavern was the only place that could truly be considered quiet.

Kneeling by the pool, Nola stared down at her reflection.

My eyes still look the same.

She smiled. Her eyes didn't brighten as they should.

Nola splashed her hands in the water to rinse them, swishing her fingers around vigorously enough that her reflection couldn't reform. Letting her hands drip dry, she jogged through the cavern to the tunnel that led to the main corridors of Nightland.

The tunnel had been left mostly to its own devices just as the cavern below had. Swatches were pure, left as the mountain had created them. Then the walls would be carved smooth for a few feet as the architects guided the path to the farm below. The steep and winding climb would have tired her legs before, but jogging up the tunnel with her bag bouncing at her side didn't even change her breathing.

Bright lights from the main corridor poured into the last few feet of the tunnel. Nola pulled the cloth from her nose, relishing her first breath of clean air.

"I was just about to send a search party down after you." Jeremy leaned against the wall, a plate of food in his hand.

Nola's mouth watered at the scent of fresh bread and cheese. "Am I running late?"

"Only about an hour." Jeremy shook his head as Nola took a giant bite of the bread.

"Sorry." She covered her mouth with her hand. "I'm not very good with time down there."

"Well, if I can ever find one, I'll snag you a watch." Jeremy winked.

Nola rose up on her toes, pressing her lips to the stubble on his cheek. "Thanks."

He wrapped an arm around her, letting her lean on his side as she downed the food.

"How was it down there?" he asked once she'd emptied the plate.

"Fine." She wrapped her arms around his waist, laying her cheek on his chest. "Stinky, quiet, I got all the samples I needed."

"Good."

"Was it not supposed to go well?"

Nola smiled as a rumble of laughter shook Jeremy's chest.

"I'm just always surprised is all." He tipped up her chin to look into her eyes. "You used to hate being underground, and now you march into the middle of a mountain every day. I'm just impressed." He kissed her gently.

Her heart skipped a beat as he lifted his face away.

"You never cease to amaze me, Nola Kent."

Nola took his hand, keeping her arm pressed to his as they walked down the hall.

"There is no aboveground here," Nola said. "Except the gardens, and only vampires are allowed out there. Besides, after everything we've seen and survived, and after that last trip through the Nightland tunnels, I guess my definition of *scary* has changed a bit."

"Last trip through the Nightland tunnels?" Jeremy asked.

"When we were running from the domes," Nola said. "Before

you found me in the city. After the tunnel I had to crawl through, the mushroom field seems huge."

Jeremy's shoulders tensed. "You went through Nightland?"

"Yeah." Nola stopped, stepping aside to let a man with a crate of food pass. "How did you think we got into the city?"

"Boats," Jeremy said. "The same way Nightland crept across to attack us."

Nola furrowed her brow, trying to remember if Jeremy had ever asked how she had gotten into the city. "There were never any boats. At least not that I saw. There was a tunnel that started in a dead tree and cut under the river. I thought the Outer Guard had found it. I thought that's how you knew we were in the city."

"We just knew Nightland had gone back over the bridge after they attacked the domes and assumed Raina would take you into the city," Jeremy said.

"You were so close to us. I heard"—a lump pressed into Nola's throat—"I heard you say you'd never stop looking for me."

Jeremy closed his eyes. "I could have found you before you got hurt."

"Shh." Nola wrapped her arms around his neck, pressing her cheek to his. "Please don't. You saved me, and we're together. And even if you had found me, the domes would have locked me up. And Salinger and the Incorporation still would have destroyed the city. And I know you, Jeremy. You wouldn't have been able to help them do that."

"No, I wouldn't." He held her tight, like he was afraid the domes could still come and rip her away.

"Then we're where we should be." Nola kissed him, letting his taste flood her mouth. "And we're together."

"I love you." He kissed the top of her head. "More than anything that has ever existed, I love you."

Nola's heart swelled, sending heat rushing to her cheeks. "I love you, too."

We could sneak away, hide where no one will find us.

"I need to turn these samples in," Nola whispered.

"We must work for science." Jeremy took her hand. "What the world needs is more mushrooms, and I think you're just the one to deliver."

"Stop it." Nola knocked her shoulder into his arm.

"Then we spar?" Jeremy asked.

"Oh yes," Nola said. "Raina laughing and telling me I'll never properly gut someone is my favorite time of day."

"It brings her inside," Jeremy said. "That's something."

Nola's joy faded away, popped like a bubble of soap she had been foolish enough to think she could hold in her hand.

"It is good for her to come in for a while," Nola said. "We all have a job to do, but…"

"Her sister isn't coming," Jeremy said.

"No, she's not."

They walked in silence until the crackling of remembered fire grew too loud in Nola's ears.

"How was Emanuel today?"

"Fine. We talked about organizing everyone for training sessions and working on drills for evacuating non-combatants in case Nightland is attacked."

"And?"

"And there's nowhere to go," Jeremy said. "Everyone could run to the mushroom farm, but there's no way to reinforce or create an exit. The survivors would end up in a siege with the guards, and there's no way Nightland would win."

Nola bit her lips together, holding her question as four children ran past. Each of them held a book in their hands.

A hope for the future if the domes will allow us to have it.

"So there wasn't any progress?" Nola stopped in front of a metal door.

"Well"—Jeremy glanced up and down the corridor—"a helicopter was spotted in the sky."

"What?" Nola squeaked. She clapped a hand over her mouth as her voice bounced down the hall.

"It took off at daybreak and flew away. There's been no sign of it since."

"What does that mean?" Nola held Jeremy's hand with both of hers, clinging on like she already knew what he was going to say.

"Not sure. Emanuel and I agree, if we don't see any movement, in two days we send scouts down to see what's happening."

"No," Nola said. "Why would anyone go down there? The only information we could gain is that we don't need to hide anymore. It's past season for the garden, we can wait—wait a month even—then see what's going on."

"What if they've brought in more guards?" Jeremy asked. "What if they're rallying guards from all over the world to attack us?"

"Does it matter?" Nola asked. "There's nowhere else for us to go. We have to stay here, so we should just stay hidden."

"If they're going to come for us, we could disband," Jeremy whispered. "Head out in small groups. They wouldn't be able to find us all, and some people might make it. If they attack while we're all here, we all die."

Nola pressed her forehead to his chest, searching for a reason to tell him he was wrong.

"If we have to run—"

"We run together," Jeremy said. "There's no question of that."

"And T and Beauford come with us," Nola said. "I won't leave them."

"I wouldn't ask you to."

"And if you go on the scouting mission to the domes"—Nola squared her shoulders—"I'm going with you."

"Absolutely not," Jeremy said.

"Then you don't go either," Nola said. "The only reason you'd be a better choice than Raina or Desmond is because you can go in the daylight. If you have to go in the daylight, you aren't going alone, which means I'm coming with you. I'm the only other superhero we've got, remember?"

Jeremy stared up at the ceiling for a long moment. "We'll just keep our fingers crossed that something will change in the next two days that will keep Nightland safe and you in the tunnels."

"Why two days?" Nola asked.

"That's when you get your last dose," Jeremy said. "I won't risk either of us going far from Dr. Wynne before you get that injection."

Pain raced through Nola's veins at the thought of the ice flooding her again.

"Right." She nodded, feeling like her head was bobbling uselessly around. "Right. Mushrooms. I should get these in to him."

"Want me to come in?" Jeremy asked.

"Better not," Nola said. "I'll meet you in the sparring room?"

"I'll be the one with the bow staff." Jeremy kissed her and left her in front of the metal door.

Nola turned the handle without knocking and stepped into Kieran's lab.

CHAPTER TWENTY

Beakers bubbled on the table, sending puffs of steam into the air. Vines grew up the far wall, their color gray though the plants thrived. Terrariums of insects lined one side of the room, while cupboards and a heavy sink stood along the other.

Kieran sat at the center of it all, hunched over a scraped up microscope that looked older than him or Nola. He glanced up for only a second when she entered his laboratory.

"I've brought all the samples," Nola said. "Things are still going well. Too bad people can't live on mushrooms alone or we'd be set for the whole winter."

"The animals can eat the extras." Kieran kept his eye pressed to his microscope. "Better to have too much than too little."

"Of course." Nola dropped her bag on the table, careful to let it fall with a *thump*.

Kieran's jaw tensed, cutting into a line that looked more statue than living.

"Do you want me to test the samples?" Nola opened the far cupboard, pulling out the giant binder that held all the data from the mushroom field experiments.

"I can do it," Kieran said. "You should go meet up with him."

"Him?" Nola dropped the binder onto the table. "You mean Emanuel, Beauford, Julian?"

"Jeremy." Kieran gripped the table, his knuckles turning white from the pressure. "You know I mean Jeremy. I could hear his voice through the door."

"You're right." Nola pulled the samples from her bag, laying them out in a long line. "Jeremy walked me here, and he's waiting for me in the sparring room. But he has practicing of his own to do, so I have time to do the work myself."

She unwrapped the first set of samples. A young button mushroom from one of the beds. "We should look at putting in more places to grow in the cavern. There's plenty of room, and it's going well."

"He could have come in with you." Kieran stood.

For a moment, Nola thought he would walk toward her, but he headed to the cupboards, pulling out a green file. He didn't say anything else as he walked past her back to his seat.

"Did you want Jeremy to come in with me?" Nola asked.

"I'm sure he'd be happier if you weren't alone with me." He scratched out notes on his paper.

"I'm surrounded by vampires all the time. I don't think you're any more likely to try and hurt me than the rest of them," Nola said.

"That's not what I mean."

"I know." Nola pulled an oyster mushroom from its wrapping. "Jeremy trusts me."

"Hmm."

"Don't *hmm*, Kieran." She pulled the glass vial from its cloth. "Just because you live in a warped little world where trust is something most people don't bother to understand doesn't mean it doesn't exist." The vial snapped. Nola gasped as shards of glass cut deep into her palm. "Dammit."

Kieran took her hand, his cold fingers touching her skin before she even knew he'd stood up.

"We need to wash out the dirt." He moved toward the sink.

"The dirt won't hurt me, Kieran."

He closed his eyes, nodding to himself before opening them again. "Right, you're right. But we at least need to pull out the glass."

His black eyes didn't turn up to her face as he ran water over her palm.

The water in Nightland held no heat. It matched the cool of the vampires' skin. Graylock hadn't stolen Nola's warmth. It had left her maddeningly close to human. Her flesh warm, feeling every chill of Kieran's touch.

"I know you trust Jeremy," Kieran said, his tone barely above a whisper. "And I want you to be right about him. I just..."

"Just what?" Nola held her hand still as Kieran pulled free the first shard of glass.

"I've loved you for a very long time, Nola. You were my whole world. Dead mom, crazy dad...you were everything to me. If I hadn't left the domes, we'd probably still be together." A smiled touched Kieran's lips.

"I never wanted you to leave." Blood dripped from Nola's hand, falling to the stone floor. "I mourned for you. It was like you died."

"Sometimes, I wished I had," Kieran said. "But Dad had a mission. He had to save people, and I had to make sure he didn't die doing it."

"He did save a lot of people."

"That's just it." Kieran finally met her gaze. "Half of Nightland wouldn't be here without him, without ReVamp. Some of the humans would be dead, too."

"And without you, what food would there be?" A tingle of something itched at the center of Nola's chest.

"Not enough to keep our people fed." Pleading filled Kieran's eyes. "The day we got kicked out of the domes was the day I lost you. And then when you came to Nightland, for one crazy moment, I thought I could have you back."

"So did I."

"But it was already too messed up, Nola. You never could have walked away until the domes made you. And you had Jeremy waiting for you and protecting you in ways I couldn't, because Nightland is my home. These are my people. They have been for a long time." He ran her hand under the water again. "But the thing is, if I could go back, I wouldn't change it. If Dad and I had stayed in the domes, a lot of people would have died because we wouldn't have been there to help."

"Kieran—"

"I love you, Nola. I will always love you, and maybe I'll never love anybody else. But I can't regret what's happened. I can't regret the Nightland I helped to build."

"What you've done is amazing." Nola touched Kieran's cheek. "If this place didn't exist, I don't know what would have happened."

He held her hand to his face. "I know I've messed up a hundred ways, and I don't know if you're ever going to be able to forgive me or trust me. But I don't think I can survive in this tomb with you hating me. And Jeremy hating me. Jeremy and I used to be friends, and...I don't know if I can be happy for you yet, but I'm going to try. And maybe someday—"

Nola wrapped her arms around his neck, laying her cheek next to his. "We'll all work on it. On trusting each other. There are only five ex-Domers here. We can't afford to hate each other."

"We can't." Kieran held her tightly. "I've really missed you, Nola."

"I've missed you too." A tear fell from Nola's cheek, mixing with the blood she'd dripped on Kieran's shoulder. "Sorry I bled on you."

"A snack for later." Kieran gave a tiny smile. "Too much?"

"Maybe a little." Nola shrugged.

The tiny tingle in Nola's heart had turned into a painful tear. "Is this supposed to hurt?"

"It hurts me," Kieran said, "but I won't keep fighting it and make you hurt more. That's all it would do, and I can't take that."

"Right." Nola rubbed her fingers over her palm. The cuts had already disappeared. "How long do you think it'll hurt?"

"For me?" Kieran turned back to his worktable. "Forever."

CHAPTER TWENTY-ONE

"You've got to pay attention," Raina growled. "Your work is sloppy."

Nola wiped the blood off her cheek. "Well, my face is bleeding."

"You'll heal." Raina prowled the inside of their sparring square.

"I also don't know what I'm doing," Nola said.

"You're distracted." Raina flipped her blade back and forth in her hand. "Distraction gets people killed. Not paying attention gets people killed."

Raina threw her knife at Nola's thigh. Nola dove to the side.

"Hey!" The shout came from behind Nola. She rolled over to see a man hopping on one leg, Raina's dagger protruding from his calf.

"What the hell do you..." his voice trailed away as his eyes found Raina's face. "Sorry." He grimaced as he pulled the knife free, carefully wiping his blood from the blade as he hobbled over to Raina. "Sorry." He passed her the blade with a bow, leaving a trail of blood behind as he limped back to his own square.

"See what happens when you don't listen, Domer?" Raina held

her blade up to the light as though inspecting it for any damage the man she stabbed might have done to it.

"I *am* listening," Nola said. "I promise I'm listening. I'm just not very good at fighting."

"Sure you are," Raina said. "Your heart just isn't in it. I heard from a little birdy you even stabbed yourself a vampire in the domes. You have to want to kill, Nola. You can't just want to learn to swing a knife around. You have to learn to *want to kill*. Now let's go again."

Raina tossed her knife into the air, letting the blade spiral before catching the hilt with a grin.

A flicker of red moved behind Raina's shoulder as Jeremy stepped away from his match to watch.

"Don't look at lover boy. Look at the one holding the knife," Raina said. "If it comes down to a fight and you worry more about where he is than who's trying to kill you, you'll end up dead. Then he'll probably end up dead because he's distracted by your death. So get your shit together and focus on not getting sliced and diced."

"Fine." Nola tightened her grip on her own blade. "Let's do this."

"Don't you sound fancy?" Raina leapt forward before she finished speaking.

Nola spun out of the way.

The hard touch of metal brushed her shoulder before she could face Raina again. Nola sliced in, aiming for Raina's thigh. Raina grabbed her wrist, smashing the knife from Nola's grip with the hilt of her blade.

"You've got to do better." Raina sauntered back to her side of the square.

Nola shook her hand out, trying to get rid of the tingling Raina's blow had left behind.

"Are you sure—" Jeremy began.

"Do you want me to be nice or do you want your lover alive?" Raina asked.

Heat flooded Nola's face. "It's fine, Jeremy. No killing each other in the sparring room. That's Emanuel's rule, right?" The powerful assent Nola had been hoping for didn't come.

"I won't kill you," Raina laughed, "but those poor people who've been assigned to the laundry, they are starting to hate all the blood stains I've been making."

You can do this, Nola. You are more than just another bloodstained shirt.

Nola took a step forward.

"Here kitty, kitty," Raina cooed.

Nola dove forward, slashing at Raina's arm.

Raina knocked her hand aside, but Nola held onto her blade.

Nola aimed for Raina's forearm. Her blade touched Raina's sleeve before Raina swung her left arm, hitting Nola hard in the elbow.

Stars danced in Nola's eyes as she stumbled aside. The glint of Raina's knife cut through her vision. Nola kicked back, catching Raina hard in the shin.

"Yes!" Jeremy's shout carried around the room.

Raina swiped a kick at Nola's ankles, knocking her face first onto the ground.

Nola coughed, dragging air back into her lungs.

"Better," Raina said. "You'd still be dead, but I'd be a little less ashamed to have known you."

"Thanks." Nola rolled onto her back. "Are you sure I shouldn't just practice with the Guard guns. I'm pretty good at those."

"We don't have the ability to manufacture the fancy little darts those guards love so much, so no." Raina kicked Nola's toes. "There will be no target practice in this apocalypse, Domer. We can sharpen blades, and, if we get really desperate, we could even make some knives. So let's stick to things your incompetence won't waste, shall we?"

"You don't have to be mean about it," Jeremy said, glaring at Raina as he lifted Nola off the floor. "She's doing really well."

"Then let her fight her own battles." Raina snatched Nola's knife from the ground. "Like it or not, we can't always be there to protect the people we care about. Better to make sure they can fight on their own."

Jeremy opened his mouth, but Nola covered his lips with her fingers.

"Leave it," Nola said. "What's the point in being a superhero if I can't take care of myself?"

Jeremy shook his head and left their square.

"Superhero?" Raina raised an eyebrow and handed Nola back her knife. "How fancy."

"Can we just get to the bit where you cut me again?" Nola asked.

"How did you know that was my favorite part?" Raina strolled back to her side of the square. "This time I want you to try and get my knife out of my grip. Don't worry about inflicting damage. Focus on disarming me."

"Right." Nola focused on the blade in Raina's hand.

Raina didn't grip the hilt as Nola clutched hers. She held her blade tenderly, like the knife was a treasure to be cherished. An extension of her arm.

Nola loosened her grip on her own blade, willing the tension out of her hand.

"Come on, we don't have all night," Raina said.

Nola lunged, swiping her blade up toward Raina's stomach. Raina's palm crashed into Nola's forearm, knocking Nola's knife hand aside.

Nola sliced her other hand up, striking Raina's wrist from below.

Raina grabbed the wrist of Nola's knife hand, twisting her arm, and pinning her blade behind her back. Pain burst from Nola's shoulder, radiating down her arm.

"And we have a dead Domer." Raina tapped her knife on Nola's jugular.

"But it was better." Nola spoke through gritted teeth. "You have to admit I'm getting better."

"Not good enough," Raina whispered in her ear. "Don't make me regret letting you out of the domes."

"I helped you escape." Nola gasped as Raina let her arm go.

"I could have left you behind," Raina said. "Let them keep you locked in a glass cage where it's safe."

Nola shook blood back into her fingers. "You wouldn't have done that. Mostly because you keep your word, even though you like to pretend you're all rogue, but a little bit because for some weird reason you like me. And you don't like many people."

Raina stared at Nola, her lips twisting into a sneer.

Feet planted and ready, knife in her hand, Nola waited for Raina to laugh or to charge and stab her in the heart.

"If you think my considering you worthy of the oxygen you consume means you're any more likely to survive with subpar fighting skills, then we might as well light your funeral pyre now," Raina said. "You can collect the wood yourself. It will save the rest of us the trouble."

Nola kept her chin up and her gaze locked with Raina's.

"Let's go again," Raina growled.

"Good." Nola softened her knees, waiting to see which direction Raina would attack.

"Raina." The young blond vampire burst through the tunnel door. "Raina, you need to come right now."

"What is it?" Raina slid her knife back into its sheath.

"I'm not sure," the girl said. "But there's a pack of them coming up the hillside."

"Dammit." Raina was through the door before she finished her curse.

Nola hesitated for only a moment before running after Raina.

"Nola!" Jeremy's footfalls thundered behind her. "What are you doing?"

"If the guards are coming to kill us all, I'd rather see what's happening than wait in the dark to die."

Jeremy slipped his fingers through hers, still holding his staff in the other hand. "If things go badly, and I say—"

"If you say run, we run," Nola said. "But if they were going to drop fire, they wouldn't be sending their own people up the mountain."

"They sent them into the city," Jeremy said. "We can't predict what they're going to do, not anymore."

Four people waited at the first window. Raina stood in front of the opening, arms crossed as she stared out into the moonlight.

"What is it?" Nola whispered.

"Zombies." Raina shook her head.

"What?" Nola peered out the window.

Halfway down the mountain, a group of six shuffled up the slope in the darkness. They didn't climb with deliberate steps as an Outer Guard, vampire, or werewolf would, nor did they stumble tiredly up the incline. Their gait lurched as they wove closer, barely avoiding ramming into the trees, their movements more like sleepwalkers than people who had deliberately chosen a path.

"I've never seen them travel in packs like that," Jeremy said. "You usually find them one at a time."

"Why are they coming up here?" Nola asked.

"Scent." Raina leaned on the window sill. "At least that's what we've found. Blind them, plug their ears, and the zombies hunt by scent."

"They're smelling Nightland?" A wave of bile surged into Nola's throat.

"Yep," Raina said. "But they can't get up here, so let the chompers hunt."

"We can't," Jeremy said. "Six moving that quickly. Most

zombies make it, what, a week after taking a bad batch of Vamp or Lycan?"

"Some make it two," Raina said. "I've seen one at three weeks, couldn't move though. Mostly just a pile of snarling goo."

Nola covered her mouth with her hand, swallowing the vomit that burned her tongue.

"If they're moving that well, chances are they injected after the fire in the city," Jeremy said. "They could still be carrying bottles with trackers hidden in them."

"And six moving together might be enough to get the domes' attention." Raina pulled her knife from her belt. "Come on, kids. Let's go kill some zombies."

"I'll come." Jeremy stepped between Nola and Raina. "Nola can go tell Emanuel what's happening."

"She comes, and that's final. She needs to start fighting for herself, and what better way to learn than with the undead?" Raina said.

"She's right," Nola said.

"You don't need to go out there and kill people, Nola," Jeremy said. "I know you need to learn to fight, but killing is different."

"They're already dead, Jeremy," Nola said. "Their bodies just haven't stopped working yet."

"You." Raina pointed to the blond who had come to the sparring room. "You've been all antsy. You get to come and be our runner."

"Really?" The girl's face lit up. "I mean"—her smile disappeared into a façade of cool indifference—"if you need someone fast, I can help you out."

"Oh joy." Raina walked down the hall, twirling her blade in her hand. "Remember, it's the head and the heart, kids. And avoid the teeth. Zombies give a nasty bite, and we don't want anyone to bleed all the way to the library on the way home from our field trip."

The weight of the blade in Nola's hand grew as they neared

the exit of Nightland. She had killed before. Her hand remembered the strength it took to drive a blade into a person's heart.

It'll be easier now. I'm strong enough to break through bones.

Her hand shook.

"You don't have to do this," Jeremy said.

"Yes, she does," Raina said.

"You can go back," Jeremy said. "Three against six is fine numbers for zombies. I'll be back in no time."

"I'm coming," Nola said. "Hiding won't stop it from happening."

"But it will keep you from remembering doing it," Jeremy said.

The back of Nola's hand brushed Jeremy's.

Agree with him. Go back.

"She needs to practice. End of discussion." Raina stopped at the ledge. "If she gets killed the first time she fights, bad memories won't matter for long."

Nola nodded, not trusting herself to say anything other than *I can't do this.*

"Keep together, and keep quiet." Raina looked to the blond. "If this is a trap and the Guard come for us, we die before we give up the location of Nightland. If anyone slips and lets the Domers know where our home is, the blood of every man, woman, and child of Nightland will be on their head."

"Death before betrayal." The blond nodded.

"Good." Raina winked at Nola and Jeremy. "Now let's get some exercise." She jumped off the ledge and moved down to the tree line.

"Why didn't she question us?" Nola whispered.

"We saw the fire packs work," Jeremy said. "Neither of us would let the domes do that again."

Nola nodded and leapt off the ledge. Her feet met the ground without bobbling. Jeremy landed at her side a moment later.

The night air held the chill of frost. The cold tickled her skin but had lost the ability to freeze her fingers. The ground crunched under her feet as they crept toward Raina.

She didn't look at Nola and Jeremy as they approached but kept her gaze toward the base of the mountain.

Raina signaled them forward.

Jeremy stepped behind Nola as the group moved down the mountainside.

Nola wanted to glance back to be sure he was still there. His boots made no noise as they crept onward.

There were no shapes moving through the woods. Nothing but the shadows of the trees.

Anything could be hiding out there.

Images of a hundred Outer Guard lurking just out of sight flashed through Nola's mind. Sweat slicked her palm. Her knife slipped in her grip.

Jeremy.

She tried to keep her eyes focused on the woods, but she still couldn't hear his boots.

She glanced back. He walked four feet behind her, his forehead tense as he searched the shadows.

Her heart slowed as she looked back to her own path.

A flutter of movement cut through the trees beyond.

Do I say something?

An arm reached out from behind a tree.

"There," Nola whispered, pointing to what she had seen.

Raina turned around, giving Nola an eye roll before following her pointing finger.

A woman with bright red hair stumbled out from behind the tree. Black and red sores covered her face and bare arms. She swayed in place for a moment, then tipped her head, her blank gaze finding Nola.

CHAPTER TWENTY-TWO

"Go on." Raina shooed Nola toward the redheaded zombie.

"I can—" Jeremy began.

"We've got a bigger one for you." Raina grinned as a man even larger than Jeremy lumbered out of the shadows. His face had been burned, whether before he injected himself or after, Nola didn't know.

Jeremy ran toward the towering zombie, his staff raised over his head as a slender female appeared from the shadows.

"Go, Domer." Raina charged toward the female.

Not giving herself time to think, Nola ran toward the redhead. The woman stumbled in Nola's direction, her jaw snapping like an animal determined to bite. Nola kept her knife near her center, ready to strike the woman in the heart.

She swiped at the woman's chest. The woman didn't try to bat the knife away or even seem to notice when the blade sliced into her skin. She seized Nola's arm in her grip, and dove her face toward Nola's wrist, gnashing her teeth.

Nola swallowed her scream and punched with her left hand, hitting the woman in the side of the head. She wasn't sure if the woman could register pain, but she stumbled at the blow. Nola kicked, swiping the woman's feet out from under her.

A rasping snarl rattled from the woman as she fell, rolling down the mountainside.

Nola chased after her.

The woman slammed into a tree with a *thud* that would have meant broken bones for a normal human. Her arms shook as she pushed herself up to her knees.

Nola kicked her, slamming her back to the ground. She raised her knife, aiming for the heart. Nola had expected her knife to meet bone and stop, or for muscle to slow the blade's momentum. But the knife sank through her back like she was nothing more than soft earth.

The woman stopped struggling and lay limp on the ground, her red hair covering her face.

A gurgling growl sounded behind Nola's shoulder.

A man in a black coat dove toward her. His teeth found her shoulder, digging deep into the muscle.

Nola screamed before she could stop herself. She grabbed the man's forehead, trying to push him away. He wrapped his arms around her, his vise-like grip pulling her closer. She stabbed, slicing into his stomach. Warm blood rained down on her leg, but her knife couldn't reach his heart.

Her fingers found his face. She pulled up, fighting to free herself from his jaw.

A flash of movement, and the man fell to the ground.

"Nola." Panic filled Jeremy's eyes. He tore the sleeve from his shirt, pressing the fabric to the bite on Nola's shoulder. "You're okay. You're going to be okay."

"Where are the others?"

Jeremy wrapped an arm around Nola as she swayed.

"We got all six," Jeremy said. "We're done here, we can go inside. Raina will deal with the trackers."

"He tried to eat me." Nola looked down at the man.

Blood covered his mouth, but the rest of his face still seemed human. Only three small sores marked his skin.

"We'll take you to Dr. Wynne, but you should be able to heal on your own." Jeremy had his arm around Nola's waist, trying to lead her back to the ledge.

Her feet wouldn't move.

The man didn't have rings under his eyes or lines on his face from a hard life on the outside. The cut of his chin, the shape of his cheeks....

"He's a Domer." Nola moved to kneel by the man, but the blood from his stomach had pooled on the frozen ground. She turned around, vomiting on the roots of a dying tree.

"Really?" Raina strolled up. "You get a little bit of blood on you and you puke?"

"He's from the domes," Nola coughed.

"Are you sure?" Raina tipped her head to the side.

"He looks familiar," Jeremy said. "I never worked with him, and he's too old to have been in our classes."

"Maintenance." Nola leaned against the tree. "He worked in maintenance. My mother hated him. He used to hum while he mopped."

"Check the others. See if you recognize them." Raina unzipped the man's shredded coat.

Nola looked away before Raina flapped it open.

Jeremy took Nola's arm as they walked toward the red-haired woman. He held her up as though he thought she might pass out at any moment.

She wanted to say thank you but couldn't find the words.

Jeremy rolled the redhead over with his foot.

Her eyes were as haunting and blank in death as they had been when she'd attacked.

"I don't recognize her," Jeremy said.

Nola shook her head, too afraid to open her mouth.

They moved on to the next. A man with dark skin and a crooked nose. Neither Nola nor Jeremy had ever seen him before.

Jeremy steered Nola away from the giant burned man. "I would have known someone that large from the domes."

"What about this one?" The blond held up a severed head.

Nola covered her eyes with shaking hands.

"No," Jeremy growled. "Now put the head down."

"Just making sure the zombie doesn't come back," the girl said.

Jeremy took Nola's hands from her face. "Last one."

A girl with blond hair lay face down on the ground, a gash sliced through her back.

Jeremy rolled her over with his foot. Her bare arm flopped to her side. There were barely any sores on her either. Only two marked her round face.

"Lilly."

Jeremy's arms wrapped around Nola before she even said her name.

"How did she get out here?"

Nola wanted to reach down and shake the girl, smack her until she woke from death and ask Lilly why she had left the domes with nothing but a bad batch of Vamp as a hope for survival.

"You know this one?" Raina said.

"She was in our class." Nola's voice shook, not with grief, but with anger. "She was in the domes when we left, and she wasn't the kind to get kicked out."

"Maybe she decided to become a rebel and left." Raina bent down, considering Lilly's corpse.

"Lilly wasn't the type for that either," Jeremy said. "She never made waves or a fuss."

"So why are they out here?" Raina asked.

"Love affair gone wrong?" the blond asked. "No one wanted them to be together so they ran away?"

"With the city burnt to the ground?" Raina pointed between Nola and Jeremy. "Not even those two are that dumb."

"Then why are they out here?" Nola asked.

"No idea," Raina said. "We need to tell Emanuel. You"—Raina turned to the girl—"search the bodies for trackers. Anything that looks strange, take it with you down to the row houses. Dump it and get back before dawn. I'll send a group out to salvage."

"Salvage?" Nola followed Raina up the slope.

"The world is ending, Domer," Raina said. "Never let a pair of good shoes pass you by."

"You're going to strip them and leave them to rot?" Nola said.

"They won't rot," Raina said. "The scavengers will eat them long before rot gets them."

"Can't we burn them?" Nola ran a few steps to catch up to Raina. Warmth squished between her toes.

"All of them or just the Domers?" Raina stopped below the ledge and rounded on Nola. "It's the circle of life. We burn our own, the rest are food for the animals. Or do those two deserve extra pity for having lived a life of privilege? Should they get better because they come from the place that just burned an entire city?"

"No." The syllable rattled in Nola's ears.

"Let's get inside," Jeremy said. "We need to talk to Emanuel and figure out what the hell is going on."

"I'll talk to Emanuel," Raina said. "You get the bloody girl cleaned up before she has a break down."

"What do you..." Nola looked down at her feet.

Blood coated her legs. Her shoes shone strangely as the red reflected the moonlight. Her fingers were stained crimson, as was the knife she still held in her hand.

The blade slipped from her grip, tumbling end over end to the ground.

"And she's gone." Raina crossed her arms.

"Nola." Jeremy tipped Nola's chin up, making her look into his eyes. "Everything is going to be okay."

"No it won't." Nola wanted to reach out and touch him, but she couldn't taint him with the death that coated her hands. "Lilly is dead, the other five are dead. Domers have gone zombie, the city is burned, and we don't know why any of this is happening."

"But we're going to figure it out," Jeremy said. "You and me together. We'll work it out, and we're going to be fine."

"You and I will." Nola stepped around Jeremy to line herself up with the ledge. "But just because we're going to be okay doesn't mean the rest of the world will be."

She jumped up, leveraging herself to land on her feet on the ledge above. Blood squelched in her shoes. She leaned over the side of the ledge and vomited again, the acid of it throttling her already raw throat.

"Are you serious?" Raina growled.

Jeremy jumped up behind her. "Let's get you inside. We'll get you into fresh clothes and—"

"Am I supposed to be good at this?" Nola searched her sleeve for a clean bit of fabric to wipe her mouth. "Do you want me to be okay with blood between my toes?"

"Never." Jeremy brushed away the curls that had pulled free from her braid. "It's not who you are. You care too much to be cold and indifferent to the pain and death around you. I will do whatever I can to make sure the world never pushes so hard you lose the ability to care for people."

"How sweet." Raina jumped up.

"Let's get you to Dr. Wynne," Jeremy said.

"Don't bother the doctor. She just needs to wash up. The skin on her shoulder's already healed. Try not to puke on anything on your way." Raina headed down the tunnel, leaving Jeremy and Nola alone in the cool night air.

"I'm not weak." Nola stared into the shadows as Raina disappeared.

Jeremy took Nola's hand, ignoring the blood on her skin. "You're the furthest from weak I could ever imagine."

They started down the hall. The wet slosh of Nola's shoes resonated off the stone walls.

"Then why do I feel like the world is going to swallow me whole?" Nola's words came out in an odd spurt as she lost the fight to keep her breathing calm.

"It won't. The world won't swallow you, Nola. It needs you too much." He kept his voice low and steady. "We need someone whose heart can still care. Still hurt for people she doesn't even know."

They walked in silence past the windows. Nola wanted to hum or scream. Anything to be sure she wouldn't hear the sounds of the girl searching through the pockets of the dead.

The door of the sparring room heaved open before they could reach it. Two men with empty crates squeezed past them in the hall.

Lilly's shoes will be worth something. Life in the domes won't have given them much wear.

Silence overtook the sparring hall in a deafening wave as Nola stepped into the room. All eyes found her, taking in her bloody legs, torn up shoulder, and deathly pale face.

Nola kept her head high as she walked through the room, carefully avoiding looking anyone in the eye.

"Her shoes." The whisper prickled the back of Nola's neck.

She turned to see who had spoken, but the path behind her drove every other thought from her mind.

Dribbles of blood stained the floor everywhere she'd stepped.

Jeremy wrapped an arm around Nola's waist, half-carrying her out of the room.

"I have to clean it up." Nola struggled against Jeremy's grip.

"Someone else can do it."

Tears blurred Nola's vision.

Raina's voice carried through the library door as they passed.

Jeremy didn't stop at the door to his room. He led her farther down, barely knocking before swinging open the door to the shower.

The small room smelled like damp stone and silt. A tap hung high on the wall.

Jeremy took the bottom of Nola's shirt, pulling it over her head before she could blink the tears from her eyes. She kicked off her shoes and socks, unwilling to touch them with her fingers.

He turned on the tap. Cool was the only temperature Nightland had to offer. Nola stepped under the water, grateful for even that thin comfort as she scrubbed her hands.

"I'll go find some clean clothes," Jeremy said.

Nola grabbed his hand before he could reach for the doorknob.

"Stay." Nola pressed her forehead to his chest. "Please stay."

Her lips found his as she pulled him into the water, grateful for the racing beat of his heart. Proof she couldn't ignore that life still existed.

CHAPTER TWENTY-THREE

"We need to know." Jeremy stood in front of Emanuel's red chair. "If there are Domers roaming outside the glass, we can't afford to hide here anymore."

Nola glanced from Jeremy to Emanuel. The tension in the air pressed against Nola's lungs. Emanuel sat with his fingers tented under his chin. Raina's hand rested on the hilt of her knife. Kieran stood with his arms crossed, looking anywhere but at Jeremy. The only one who seemed at ease was Julian.

"What would there be to find out?" Kieran asked. "If they're coming for us, they'll come. If they've kicked out some of their own people, it doesn't affect us."

"It does." Nola tucked her damp curls behind her ears. "Something is wrong with the domes. Salinger may be a demon, but he wouldn't go around kicking people out. They're needed to maintain the population. The guards that were killed threw off the numbers. Jeremy and I leaving did, too. They wouldn't just let people leave."

"They've just brought in a massive amount of Outer Guard," Emanuel said. "Perhaps they've decided they have no further use for a civilian population."

"Even in Nightland someone cleans the floors and does the laundry," Raina said. "You'd have to be desperate to get rid of the guy who mops."

"Fair enough," Emanuel said. "But if the domes have lost their minds and started getting rid of their own, it only gives me more reason to keep my people safe within Nightland's walls."

"Not if Salinger has taken over." Jeremy glanced around the room. "Is there someplace else we could talk about this?"

Emanuel's gaze traveled from Julian to Raina and Kieran before fixing on Nola. "We could go to my kitchen if you like, but all of these people will come with us."

Jeremy bit his lips together. "There's a reason people don't talk about Salinger. I barely know anything about him, and I was a guard. He's the side of the domes none of the Domers want to talk about. He's basically the boogey man. He's vicious, was vicious enough with the outsiders at his home domes he got a reputation for being brutal. The Incorporation wanted to send him here a few years ago when the riots started to get bad. My father said no."

"What?" Nola stepped up next to Jeremy.

"It was right after your dad died," Jeremy said. "We needed help, but my dad knew Salinger would just make things worse. He told the Incorporation he had his own plans."

"Graylock," Kieran said.

"A way to keep the Incorporation and Salinger as far away from here as possible." Julian leaned against a bookcase, mug in hand. "It's rather brilliant. Where I come from, they welcomed Salinger with open arms. He was much younger then, though I'm not sure if time will have made him better or worse. He stripped down the community outside our domes to the bare minimum for keeping the useful factories running. Everyone else was given three days to clear out of the area or risk the wrath of the domes. I left the domes and blended in with the others who were fleeing. Most of those poor people didn't last two weeks once the city had been closed to them. The man has no mercy."

"We already figured that out when he slaughtered a city full of people," Raina said. "So why are we still talking about this?"

"Because it doesn't make sense," Jeremy said. "Either Salinger is in control of the domes and is kicking people out, in which case we need to get as far away from here as we can. Or there's something else wrong with the domes."

A knot of fear pinched between Nola's shoulder blades.

"What do you mean *wrong*?" Raina asked.

"If the domes have fallen." Julian set down his mug. "The domes are a delicate ecosystem. Everything must be in perfect order for life to continue. When I was part of the domes, I was an asset manager. Every item the domes utilized had been decided long before I took my post, and there was no room for error or short falls. Maintaining the operation of the domes was a worry constantly haunting all our dreams."

"The domes were built to run for generations." Fear twisted a path down Nola's spine.

"Absolutely," Julian said. "If everything goes well, the domes could be self-sustaining for hundreds of years. But if the population were to decrease or increase too drastically, there would either be a work shortage or a food deficit. A fungus could wipe out the food supplies, an issue with the cooling systems could destroy all of the seeds."

"If life in the glass is always on the verge of collapse, why didn't they tell us?" Nola asked.

"We were kids," Kieran said. "Why would you tell kids they might not get to grow up?"

"The domes demand certainty," Emanuel said. "You started to doubt, and look where it led you."

"How much harder would it be to invest yourself in the mission of the domes if you weren't sure the mission would succeed?" Julian asked.

"So the two theories we're going with are a psychopath has taken over the domes," Nola said, "or the domes have fallen?"

"Can you think of another option?" Emanuel asked.

Nola's mind raced, searching through every possibility. "What if Lilly decided she couldn't stay in the domes after they burned the city? What if she couldn't live with the guilt?"

"Do you really think Lilly would have done that?" Pity filled Jeremy's eyes.

Nola rubbed her hands over her face. "No, she wouldn't."

"Emanuel," Jeremy said. "Something is going on out there. We need to know what it is."

Emanuel stared at Jeremy for a long moment. "The five of you go. Take the sun suits and whatever weaponry you need. Find out what you can, and come back alive. Don't let anyone follow you home."

"Nola should stay behind," Jeremy said.

"I'm going." Nola laid her hand on his arm. "Don't fight me on it."

"Not until you get your last dose," Kieran said. "Dad won't allow it."

"Then I'll take it now." Nola walked toward the back door of the library. "One day early can't hurt, right?"

"Nola, we don't know what will happen if you take it early." Jeremy chased after her.

"You got a shot in the stomach when you almost died," Nola said. "That was less than two weeks. They did it for you. Dr. Wynne can do it for me."

Nola strode through the door.

Eden pouted at the kitchen table. Bea sat across from her, glowering at Eden as she pushed food around her plate.

"Eden." Nola stopped in the doorway, the desire to hold the child just to prove the little girl was alive pressed painfully in her throat. "What's wrong with your food?"

Eden looked at Bea, then back down at her plate. "Daddy said he would sit with me while I ate."

"We had to talk to him in the library." Nola knelt next to Eden's chair. "It's hard when your parent has a lot of responsibility."

Eden's bottom lip trembled. "I want daddy."

"I know." Nola tucked Eden's dark hair behind her ears. "But you know what we were talking about? Keeping you and everybody who lives here safe. I'm sorry he missed dinner, but he's trying to take care of you as best he can. Okay?"

Eden nodded.

"You know how you could help him?" Nola asked.

Eden shook her head.

"Eat up all your food so you can stay nice and strong." Nola pushed Eden's plate toward her. "That would be a really big help."

Eden narrowed her eyes at her roasted mushrooms and squash. "I want to help." She picked up a mushroom and tucked it into her mouth.

"Good job." Nola stood and walked out into the hall.

"Nola?" Eden's voice pulled her back. "My daddy will take care of you, too."

"He will." Nola nodded, pressing her face into a careful smile.

"Nola," Jeremy whispered behind her shoulder.

"What?" She stopped at the big metal door.

"We could wait another day," Jeremy said. "If you're really determined to go—"

"How many more people could take bad Vamp in a day?" Nola asked. "I don't want to have to stab someone I know in the heart. You said I'm strong, Jeremy. I don't know if I'm strong enough for that."

She knocked on the laboratory door.

"Come in," Dr. Wynne's cheerful voice called back.

Before Nola had pushed the door fully open, Dr. Wynne was on his feet.

"Nola." He held out his hands in greeting. "I was told you had been bitten, but I don't think there's anything I can do for you. Jeremy." He added the less enthusiastic greeting as Jeremy stepped into the room.

"I'd like my last injection." Nola sat on the table. "It's only a day early, and I need to leave for a little while."

"Leave?" Dr. Wynne blinked at her. "Leave for where?"

"It's a long story," Jeremy said. "We shouldn't be gone long, in fact we can wait—"

"Jeremy." Nola spoke his name as a warning.

"I can give you the shot now." Dr. Wynne moved to his table in the corner where a cold storage box hummed dully. "I'm not sure if it will reduce its effectiveness, though it certainly shouldn't damage you."

"Reduce its effectiveness?" Jeremy asked.

"Healing and the like," Dr. Wynne said. "I'm not sure if the dose will remain as effective in the long run. I'm afraid I just don't have the data to make an accurate assessment."

"We already know I heal just fine from zombie bites." Nola unbuttoned the top of her shirt. "If I get really hurt, we can give me another dose then."

"Well, yes." Dr. Wynne lifted a black-filled syringe from the box. "We are working with a limited supply, of course. We've only got two full doses after this. I've been using one to study the formula."

Nola gripped the edge of the metal. The bottom lip of the table hadn't been filed down. The sharp edges dug into her fingers.

"You can't make any more?" Jeremy asked.

"I could," Dr. Wynne said. "It's not that difficult, really. I could make more of it right here, if I had the formula. Right now, I'm working my way backwards. Think of it as baking bread, if you will. I know I need flour, leavening, salt, but the exact recipe is very difficult to find. That's how we end up with so many bad batches of Vamp and Lycan. Without the exact details, the results can be deadly. In time, perhaps I would be able to come up with the right process, but it could take years."

"Then you can't go." Jeremy took Nola's hands. "You have to stay here and safe."

Nola pressed her fingers to his lips. "I can heal. We've seen it. If someone ripped out one of our jugulars, we'd still heal. It would take time, but I could keep you safe. And I know you would do the same for me."

"But—"

Nola leaned into Jeremy, pressing her lips to his.

"This makes going to the city even more important than before," Nola said. "The city is one small river away from the domes. Graylock was made in the labs there. If the domes really are falling apart, the formula could be lost forever. Let's find the bread recipe and bring it back."

"And if Salinger is still there?" Jeremy asked.

"We let Raina kill him," Nola said.

"I would suggest taking one spare dose with you and leaving the rest here for me to continue my work." Dr. Wynne stepped up to Nola, needle in hand. "Then, if this doesn't work as planned, you can give Nola the extra dose."

"I won't need it." Nola closed her eyes as Dr. Wynne opened her shirt.

She didn't gasp as the needle pierced her heart or scream as the ice raced down her veins.

Her blood greeted the cold as an old friend, welcoming it into every part of her.

"You'll be as strong as the drug can make you now." Dr. Wynne's words floated from far away. "So do try not to break anything."

"Breathe," Jeremy said.

Nola inhaled. Air flew into her lungs, sending power through her muscles like zaps of electricity.

The sound of crumpling metal came from beneath her.

"Oh dear," Dr. Wynne said.

"Careful." Jeremy's hands touched hers. The texture of his fingers sent chills flying up her arms.

She gasped and opened her eyes.

Blood dripped from her fingers. She let go of the table. Handprints dented the metal, and blood stained the edges.

"Here you are." Dr. Wynne passed her a wet towel.

She wiped the blood from her fingers with the cool cloth. The prefect skin on her hands held no trace of where she'd sliced open her fingers only moments before. She grabbed the edge of the table, squeezing the place where she'd already left handprints until she felt the metal cut her skin.

Holding her hands up to her face, she watched the skin knit back together as drops of blood trailed down her palm.

"This is amazing," Nola said. "I really am like a superhero."

"Superheroes can still get killed." Jeremy caught her hands as she reached toward the edge of the table again. "You have to remember that, Nola. There are some things we can't come back from."

Nola wiped the blood from her hands. "I know we can get hurt, just the same as vampires and wolves, but this is still amazing."

"Quite." Dr. Wynne handed the black case to Jeremy.

"Thank you." Jeremy slid the case onto his belt.

"Try not to need the dose, either of you." Dr. Wynne waved them toward the door.

"Dr. Wynne." Nola turned back as Jeremy stepped into the hall. "Thank you for trying with the Graylock. Your helping us means a lot."

"Well"—Dr. Wynne fluttered his hands in the air—"it is my duty as a doctor, and it could help save many more lives. Besides, you're both good people. The world needs as many of those as it can come by these days."

CHAPTER TWENTY-FOUR

Raina had cleared the sparring room, sending the fifty-odd fighting vampires scurrying into the tunnels of Nightland.

Julian pulled open the weapons cage, narrowing his eyes as he touched the hilt of each sword.

Raina reached into the other side of the cage.

"Here." She tossed Nola a belt with two knives in leather sheathes and an Outer Guard gun hanging off the side. "Remember, the pointy end goes into the people we don't like, and the bang bang stick doesn't get pointed at our friends."

"Thanks." Nola wrapped the belt around her middle.

"You almost look a little dangerous." Raina smiled.

"I'll take that as a compliment," Nola said.

"Good." Raina dug deeper into the weaponry. "Looking the part is half the battle. And for lover boy." She pulled his own Guard belt from the depths of the shelf.

"And here I thought you'd burned it." Jeremy's face betrayed no emotion as he fastened his belt around his waist.

"It still fits." Raina winked.

"I need more ammunition," Jeremy said, "and some knives wouldn't go amiss either."

Raina pulled out two smaller knives in sleek leather sheaths. She tossed one to Jeremy before tucking the other into her boot.

"Do we need packs?" Nola asked. "If we're going to be hiding during the daylight, Jeremy and I will at least need food and water."

"Who said anything about hiding?" Kieran came in from the tunnels, two wooden boxes balanced in his arms.

"I've seen what happens when vampires go into the sun, Kieran," Nola said. "None of you can risk that."

"We'll be fine." Kieran yanked the lid off the first, larger box.

"Sun suits?" Jeremy peered down at the wide brimmed hats and neatly folded stacks of tan material. "Those are sun suits from the domes."

Nola pulled out one of the jumpsuits. She'd never held one before. The coarse material itched her skin and, even with her new strength, weighed twice what she'd expected.

The sun suits were only used by the maintenance workers of the domes when they had to spend hours outside working on the air ducts, cisterns, and other external assets. Normal Domers were never outdoors long enough to need the suits, and Outer Guard uniforms had their own sun protection.

"How did you get these?" Nola asked.

Kieran opened the second smaller box. Ammunition packs of the tiny metal darts needed for the Guard guns filled the crate.

Jeremy whistled.

"You wanted to know what we couldn't ask the domes for," Kieran said. "This is what we needed."

"You broke into the domes for sun suits and ammunition?" Nola dug her fists into her eyes. "How many people died so you could have these?"

"So we could defend ourselves in the daylight?" Raina asked. "Far fewer than the domes would kill if they found us here."

"We gained a few other assets as well," Julian said. "Emanuel planned very carefully for the things we would need."

Raina took the suit from Nola, curling her lip as she shook out the fabric. "Leave it to Domers to make something so horribly unattractive."

"They'll keep us alive." Kieran pulled his suit on over his dark pants and shirt. The baggy tan fabric made him look younger, softening the hard lines the outside world had carved into him.

An old pain tugged at Nola's chest.

"Are you sure they'll work?" Jeremy asked.

"Of course." Julian tucked his brown gloves into his sleeves and took a wide-brimmed hat from the box. A tube of fabric hung from the hat, ready to cover everything but the vampires' eyes.

"I really hate these things." Raina fastened her belt on the outside of her suit. The effect was comical, like a child playing in grownups' clothes.

"So, you really are going?"

Nola spun toward T's voice. She and Beauford stood in the tunnel, Emanuel right behind them.

"We have to." Nola reached for T as she crossed into the sparring room.

T stopped to look in both boxes before taking Nola's hands.

"Why?" T asked.

"We need to know what's happening," Nola said. "We'll be back soon."

"I want to believe you," T said.

"If they say they have to go, they have to go." Beauford laid a hand on T's shoulder. "Fussing won't help anything."

T opened her mouth, then chewed her lips together and shook her head.

"Do you have everything you need?" Emanuel stepped forward to join the group.

"Weapons, sun suits, Domers." Raina counted them off on her gloved fingers. "We should be set."

"Go in and come back," Emanuel said. "If you don't have to go near anyone, don't. If you do—"

"Kill them?" Raina said.

Nola gripped the knives on her hips.

"If you have to." Emanuel took Raina's hands in his. "You have my trust, old friend. You command with my voice."

Raina bowed her head.

"Don't let them take you from me again," Emanuel said.

"I won't," Raina said.

"We should let them leave." Emanuel turned to T and Beauford. "There's only a few hours left until morning."

Tears pooled in the corners of T's eyes. "Don't let her die, Jeremy. You have to bring her back here."

In two quick steps, Nola threw her arms around T's neck. "I'm coming back. I'm going to be with you when the baby's born, I promise."

"Good." T squeezed Nola, then stepped back, looping her arm through Beauford's.

"See you soon." Beauford gave a quick nod and led T back into the tunnel.

"I expect you back by tomorrow morning." Emanuel gave each of them a long look before walking away.

Nola stood frozen, watching them all disappear from view.

"That bastard," Nola said.

"We'll be back soon." Jeremy wrapped his arms around her.

"Yeah." Nola swiped the tears from her cheeks. "Using a pregnant girl to make sure we don't jump ship. That's a really low blow."

"Would you have left?" Kieran asked.

Jeremy's arms tensed around Nola.

Nola dug her fingers into her curls. "I'm a superhero, you're a vampire, and I'm in borrowed shoes because mine got soaked through with zombie blood. Let's just go and find out if the boogey man is hiding in the domes."

"Sounds like a good time." Raina shoved open the door to the outer tunnel. "We run fast and we run silent. Last one to the city limits is zombie food." With a grin, she took off down the tunnel.

"I'll take the rear." Julian bowed the rest forward, checking the sword he'd fastened over his tan suit.

"You next." Jeremy pointed to Kieran.

"Then Nola?" Kieran asked.

Jeremy gave a nod so small it looked like a twitch.

Kieran nodded back, his eyes sweeping over Nola before he ran down the tunnel.

She chased after him, exhaling all the air from her lungs, wishing she could squeeze the air from her whole body. That she could freeze in a void with nothing to fear and nothing to care for.

Kieran ran twenty feet ahead of her, slowing and hastening his pace to match hers. Jeremy's boots thudded steadily behind her.

She had lost her dome clothes and shoes. Everything she wore had been someone else's, but Jeremy still wore his boots.

Raina dropped from the ledge as it came into view. Kieran leapt out of sight. Nola didn't hesitate to jump when her turn came.

Hitting the ground didn't break her stride.

She kept her eyes fixed on Kieran's back as they ran past the bodies of the zombies they'd ended only a few hours before.

Ended. So simple. So true.

Everything would end.

Her legs moved faster than they had when she and Jeremy had run into the city. The Graylock had finished its work. Her toes barely touched the ground as she sprinted down the mountain. She longed for her lungs to burn or her legs to ache.

End. If the domes had ended, then anything could.

The gleaming beacon of safety. The hope all the world had been told to look to as a future for the human race.

Or Salinger had stayed, ruling the domes with a fist drenched in blood. Destruction or contamination.

Which would leave more survivors?

She left her hands at her sides as she ran through the field of briars, relishing each tear of her flesh. Knowing she would be healed before she could lift her hands to see the cuts.

Death for many, or power for a devil.

Either way, the world is ending.

Raina led them out of the field and into the trees. Fresh footprints marked the dirt, leading north, away from the mountain to somewhere Nola had never seen.

I hope they survived. Wherever they are.

A voice that sounded terribly like Jeremy's echoed in the back of her mind. *If they survive, they'll live to be our enemies.*

Tears touched Nola's cheek, freezing in the cold night air.

The plants will be dead by now. T will have to live off mushrooms for the winter.

Anger burst into flames in Nola's chest, pushing her legs to run faster. But the speed didn't hurt. Running couldn't burn away her rage.

Rundown houses came into view, like slumping giants sagging from years of sadness.

Someone had built those homes. Lived in them. Children had been raised and deaths mourned within those walls.

None of it matters now. It's all just rot.

Kieran reached back, wrapping an arm around her waist before Nola could run past him.

He clapped his hand over her mouth before she could speak.

"Look." His breath whispered over her ear.

A light burned in the window of the house in front of them.

Raina stood in the middle of road, a knife in each hand. Her head swiveled slowly from side to side as though she were scenting the wind.

Nola nodded and stepped away from Kieran, reaching for her own knives.

Jeremy's fingers grazed her wrist.

Nola glanced over her shoulder.

Jeremy shook his head.

Julian's sword rasped as he pulled the long blade from its sheath.

Jeremy let go of Nola, pulling his gun from its holster. He touched the black case on his hip before raising the gun, pointing it toward the house with the light.

Raina stalked slowly toward the house, placing one foot in front of the other as though she were walking on ice.

Like people used to do on the outside. When the world would freeze them for months at a time. When life could disappear with a crack in the ice.

Raina stopped in front of the porch.

Jeremy slunk in front of Nola, pressing his back to the doorjamb, gun raised and pointing toward the closed door.

Kieran leaned against the other side, his daggers poised to strike.

Julian took Nola's shoulders, pulling her to Jeremy's side of the door as Raina nodded and leapt forward, kicking through the door with a *crack*.

Screams echoed from inside the house.

"Don't move and I don't slice, got it?" Raina said.

Nola leaned toward the door. Jeremy shot one arm back, pressing her against the wall.

"Please don't kill us!" a woman shrieked.

"That's a good start," Raina said. "Now let's get to the bit where you all stand against the wall with your arms over your head and we'll be in great shape."

"I won't be told what to do," a young man shouted.

Be good. Do what she says and be good.

Nola leaned into Jeremy's arm.

"Just do it, you fool," a woman said.

"That's better," Raina said. "See how easy it is to get along when you all do what I say?"

Kieran nodded toward the door.

Jeremy moved his arm, freeing Nola from the wall. Gun steady, he walked into the house.

Nola stepped forward to follow him.

Kieran shook his head and disappeared through the door.

"We're not here to hurt anyone." Kieran's voice carried from inside the house. "All we want is to ask a few questions and we'll be on our way."

Raina's laugh shook the cracked window panes.

Nola looked behind to Julian. He scanned the street before nodding.

She hadn't noticed she'd been holding her breath until she stepped through the doorway.

A table with four candles threw a flickering light across the room.

Four people stood pressed up against the wall: the young boy Jeremy had carried from the flames, flanked by the three women from the group that had attacked Jeremy.

Nola pulled her knives from their sheaths. "There should be more."

CHAPTER TWENTY-FIVE

"What do you mean *more?*" Raina held the tip of her knife to the boy's heart.

"When we saw those ladies last time, they had kids and two other men with them," Nola said.

"He'd been with a group in the city." Jeremy pointed to the boy. "We told them to run for it. Found him on the ground on our way out and carried him from the smoke."

"That was you?" the boy cocked his head to the side. "Where's the rest of my family?"

"We didn't see any of them," Nola said. "They left you in the middle of the road. I don't know where they went from there."

"You're lying." The boy shook his head so violently Raina's knife pierced his chest. Red blossomed on his filthy shirt. "They would never abandon me."

"People are shit, kid. Get used to it," Raina said. "Now where are the others?"

"There's no one else here," one of the women said. Her gaze darted through the shield of her dark scraggly hair toward the stairs.

"Liar," Raina whispered. "Kieran, Jeremy, sweep upstairs. If anyone is hiding up there, kill them."

"Wait!" the gray-haired woman yelped.

"Something you want to tell me?" Raina raised her other blade to the woman's neck.

"There's a little girl up there, but no one else," the gray-haired woman said. "She's just a child, please don't hurt her."

"Go." Raina nodded to Kieran and Jeremy.

"Please," the gray-haired woman murmured. "Don't kill my baby."

"I'm a vampire, not a Domer," Raina said. "I'm not in the habit of murdering children."

Kieran disappeared one way at the top of the stairs and Jeremy the other.

"What about the two men and the other child?" Nola asked, keeping her ears focused on the sounds of Jeremy's and Kieran's footsteps overhead.

"Jeffy died," the red-haired woman finally spoke. "Got into a fight that first night. Lou took the other kid and bolted. We tried to look a bit, but there were too many people running around out there. We had to stay hidden."

"Next time you decide to hide, don't leave a light on," Raina said.

"We can't see in the dark," the scraggly woman said. "We aren't like you."

"Pity," Raina said. "You'd be more likely to survive."

"It's okay," Kieran cooed from the top landing. "I'm not going to hurt you."

Sniffles sounded under his words.

He stepped onto the landing, holding a tiny girl in his arms. "We're going to take you down to sit with the others, that's all. We're making sure you're nice and safe."

"The rest is clear." Jeremy stepped out of the shadows.

"Make sure there's nothing else of interest," Raina said.

Jeremy slipped back out of sight.

"Please don't take our supplies." The redhead tipped her chin up, as though preparing to be hit. "We barely have anything. If you take our food, you might as well kill us."

The little girl began to cry.

"Shh." Kieran rocked the child. "You're okay."

The child buried her filthy face in his shoulder.

"We aren't interested in your food," Raina said. "We want information. Tell us everything we want to know, and we'll walk right back out of here, and you can go back to sitting around your candles like a pack of fools."

"What do you want to know?" the gray-haired woman asked.

"What's happened since the city burned?" Raina asked.

"We were up the hill by the time most made it out of the city," the gray-haired woman said. "That's when your friend upstairs killed one of us."

"Your friend pulled a gun on us when we were trying to help you." Nola tightened her grip on her knives. "Your *friend* shot Jeremy. You're lucky we let the rest of you run away."

The gray-haired woman glared at Nola.

"What happened after your failed attempt at murdering Jeremy and Nola?" Julian asked from his place in the door. He had his sword drawn as he faced out into the night.

"We went into one of the houses to hide," the redhead said. "We stayed in there for a couple of hours. Wanted to make sure no one was coming after us. Then we heard people coming up the road in groups."

"What kind of groups?" Kieran asked.

"Some people alone, a few groups of fifteen or twenty," the scraggly woman said. "Probably saw about three hundred people pass."

"Some of them tried to come into the house where we were hiding," the gray-haired woman said. "Jeffy tried to get them out. That's when he got killed."

"We ran," the redhead said. "Came up here to the end of the houses. Most of the ones closer to the city already had people holed up in them. Some people went into the woods, but I don't know what they think they'll find there."

The floor upstairs groaned. Jeremy stepped back out onto the landing. "Where did you get these?" He held up two dome-issued water bottles. "You were away from the city before the Outer Guard started handing these out."

"Pulled them off some bodies," the scraggly woman said. "Found a few that had been killed but still had bottles and a bit of food. It wasn't stealing. The dead don't need water."

"Have you seen any Outer Guard?" Nola asked.

"Not since I was in the city," the boy said. "I saw the ones who told us to stay put, then I woke up on the old highway. There were some people left around me. Told me the Outer Guard had taken off back across the river."

"How did you end up with them?" Raina asked.

"Knew his mother and saw him trying to go off into the woods to find her," the gray-haired woman said. "No one who's gone into those woods is still alive. People can't survive out there. It's just not possible."

"You're very clever," Raina said.

"I've heard rumors," the scraggly woman said. "Met two children headed out to the forest. They said the guards have been lurking around the city. I don't know what they're looking for, but no one in their right mind would go back in there. Took nearly a week for the smoke to stop. There's nothing of worth left in the city. Going in there is as close to suicide as going out into the woods."

"They're in there looking for more people to kill." Anger filled the boy's sallow face. "They told us to stay on that street so we would burn. Now they're going through killing anyone the smoke didn't get."

"The men who told you to stay put, what exactly did they say?

How many of them were there?" Jeremy came down the steps, his gun still in his hand.

"There were five," the boy said. "One of them shouted at us, told us to follow. That was a girl, but the four men, they all did as she said. Some ran in front of us and some in back. It felt like they were trying to protect us. We ran with them for a bit. Then guns started firing. The woman told us to run down the street and wait, said she'd be right back for us. They never came back. They left us there to die. I didn't think she'd do that. She seemed nice."

"Who was firing the guns?" Julian asked.

"The female guard, did you see her face?" Jeremy stepped closer to the boy.

The boy leaned back against the wall. "All of them had helmets on. She was taller than me. I only knew she was a girl because of her voice. Even her name didn't sound like a girl's. But I've never heard of any kind of a Gentry before."

Nola stepped between Jeremy and the boy before she knew she'd asked her feet to move.

"Where did she go?" Jeremy bumped into Nola, knocking her into the boy as he reached forward to shake him.

"Back down." Kieran grabbed Jeremy's shoulder.

Jeremy glared at him.

"Jeremy," Nola whispered.

He looked into Nola's eyes. His anger changed to fear as he saw her mashed between him and the boy. He shook Kieran's hand off and stepped back.

"Where did she go?" Jeremy said.

"Toward the shooting." The boy held his chin high.

"Where was the shooting?" Nola asked. "Which part of the city were they heading toward?"

"The old Vamper section of town," the boy said.

"Did you see any other guards while you were waiting for Gentry to come back?" Kieran asked.

The boy shook his head. "Just the ones who left us to die."

"She didn't—"

"Don't." Nola pressed her hands to Jeremy's chest.

"What about the others around here?" Raina asked. "You've just been playing decaying house for a few days. No one's come by? No more people hunting for a nice place to stay?"

"There were whole streams of people the first few days," the gray-haired woman said. "It's died down a bit. I think either folks are already dead or they've found a place to settle."

"Maybe some have found their way to you," the scraggly woman said. "Wherever you are has got to be pretty nice. Vampers and humans living together. All of you look fed and healthy. Where have you been hiding out?"

"Don't even bother," Raina laughed. "You're not invited to the party."

"What about my baby?" the gray-haired woman asked. "You had food before, you're still doing well. Surely you can help a little girl."

The little girl turned her head, pressing her cheek to Kieran's chest.

"We can't help you." Kieran set the child down.

"I would advise you put your lights out," Julian said. "And stay here as long as your supplies will last. The longer you hold out before searching for a more sustainable option, the fewer you'll have to compete with."

"You're just like them," the boy said. "Leaving us in the middle of a fire."

"Gentry wouldn't do that," Jeremy said.

"Don't start that pity party with me," Raina said. "You aren't ours to care for. One of yours tried to kill one of mine. You should feel pretty damn lucky I'm walking away without having a snack. So all of you scurry up the stairs and lock yourselves in while we wander away. If you're really lucky, I won't tell any creepy crawlies where you're hiding."

"How long do you think we'll make it?" the redhead asked. "Would it really make a difference if you killed us now?"

"Probably not," Raina said. "But I'm giving you a chance to fight. Believe me, that's something."

"It's really not," the boy said.

"We should be on our way," Julian said.

"Go," Raina ordered the group.

The gray-haired woman snatched up the little girl and ran up the stairs. The other two women were right behind her, and the child began to cry as they disappeared from sight.

The boy didn't move.

"Get upstairs," Kieran said.

"Or you'll kill me?" the boy said. "You could light the house on fire as soon as you step outside."

"I carried you from the city," Jeremy said. "I could have left you there to die, but I didn't. Don't make me regret saving you."

"Why not? I do." The boy stepped toward Jeremy.

"Raina, we need to go," Julian said.

"I don't have time for this." Raina ran her blade along the boy's shoulder, slicing through his shirt and into his skin.

The boy howled with pain.

"Run," Raina growled.

The boy dodged around her and tore up the stairs, pressing his hand to his bleeding arm.

"I hate teenagers," Raina said.

"Thanks," Nola said.

She started for the door, lining up behind Kieran.

A *thwack* and a grunt sounded from in front of her.

"Kieran!" Her shout was swallowed by Kieran's voice.

"Get him inside! Raina, come on!" Kieran leapt over something and ran into the night.

"Shit." Raina knocked into Nola as she followed Kieran out the door.

"Nola, get back." Jeremy shoved her against the wall and

reached down, seizing Julian's hands and dragging him into the house.

Blood pooled on Julian's stomach, surrounding an arrow that had pierced his suit and body.

"How?"

Jeremy ignored Nola, pulling Julian away from the door before grabbing the shaft of the arrow and yanking it from Julian's stomach.

Julian coughed. Blood spattered his veil. "I suppose I should thank you for that."

CHAPTER TWENTY-SIX

"We need to put pressure on it." Nola leaned over Julian, pressing her hands to his wound.

Julian grunted in pain, his eyes rolling back in his head.

Jeremy slammed the remains of the shattered door shut and crawled to the window, peering out into the darkness.

"What happened?" Nola asked.

"I was shot with an arrow," Julian wheezed.

"By who?" Nola asked.

The arrow lay on the floor where Jeremy had tossed it aside. Blood slicked the arrowhead and the start of the wooden shaft. The tip of the arrow had been carved from rock and faded feathers adorned the end.

"I'm almost impressed." Julian reached for the arrow. "You remove all hope and still life finds a way."

"Just breathe, Julian." Nola kept her hands pressed to the wound. "You're going to be just fine."

"I'm sure I will," Julian said. "But in the meantime, this is a bit excruciating."

"Did you see which way they went?" Jeremy kept his eyes focused on the darkness beyond the window.

"No, I was too busy looking at the arrow in Julian's stomach."

"Blow out the candles," Jeremy said.

"I can't move," Nola said.

"Don't worry about me." Julian shooed her away.

Nola crawled toward the candles, blowing each of them out in turn.

Her heart forgot to beat for a moment as the last candle went out and sense told her darkness would envelop her. But the faint light coming in from the window was enough for her eyes to see a face appear at the top of the stairs.

"Get back in the room or Jeremy shoots you," Nola said.

The boy glared at her for a moment before running away.

"They should be back by now," Jeremy said. "One person with a bow, that shouldn't give Raina any trouble."

"Unless there were more of them." Nola wiped the blood from her hands on the side of the couch, leaving streaks of red across the frayed fabric.

They sat in silence for a long moment. The faint shuffle of footsteps creaked upstairs.

"Should we go out after them?" Nola whispered.

"We're not splitting up," Jeremy said. "And we can't leave Julian behind."

"How very kind," Julian said.

"How long until you can move?" Nola asked.

Julian shifted his weight from side to side. "A few more minutes, and I should be able to stand. Might be an hour before I can fully run."

"If he can stand, you can carry him," Nola said.

"I don't believe that's the best idea," Julian said.

"Fine," Nola said. "I'll carry you. Jeremy's better with a gun."

"But where would we go?" Julian grimaced as he eased himself up onto his elbows. "I don't think there's anything to do but wait for them to come back."

"And if they don't come back?" Jeremy asked.

"They will," Julian said. "You need only give Raina time."

"How much time?" Nola asked. "They could be hurt."

"Shh," Jeremy hushed. He tipped his head, leaning closer to the windowsill.

Nola froze. Even her heart seemed to slow as she stared at Jeremy.

The floorboards above them creaked. A bedspring squeaked as someone sat down.

Outside, the dead leaves rustled, a branch cracked, someone grunted.

"Jeremy!" Nola screamed his name as the window shattered.

He covered his face as glass showered over him. A rock thumped onto the floor, rolling and settling by Nola's hands.

"Stay down!" Jeremy leapt through the broken window and out of sight.

"Help me up." Julian rolled over. His hands fumbled on the shattered glass, but still he pushed himself up to his knees.

"He said to stay down." Nola crawled to Julian's side.

"If we're being attacked, I'd prefer to be on my feet," Julian said.

Nola wrapped her arm around Julian, hoisting him up.

A *pop* sounded from the street followed by a scream of pain.

"Jeremy." Nola moved toward the shattered window.

"No!" Julian reached for her arm a moment too late.

A *whizzing* cut through the darkness. Nola twisted away from the window. Pain cut deep into her back.

"Nola!"

A *crunch* and a *thud* sounded on the street.

"Are you injured?" Julian grabbed her hand, pulling her away from the window.

"I'm fine."

An arrow stuck out of the wall right behind where Nola had been a moment before.

"Nola." Jeremy's boots thundered up the porch steps.

She twisted out of Julian's grip.

Jeremy leapt through the window and had Nola's face in his hands a moment later. "You're safe." Blood marked his cheeks, remnants of wounds that had already healed.

"It just got my back," Nola said.

Jeremy stepped around her, examining the place where the arrow had grazed her. "Dammit."

"Is it bad?" Nola asked.

"It was very nearly worse." Julian leaned against the wall.

"What happened out there?" Nola asked.

"Two new dead bodies." Raina stepped through the window, sunhat in hand, her windswept hair and the blood dripping from her blade the only signs she'd been fighting.

"Where's Kieran?" Nola asked.

"Stashing the dead men's loot to carry home." Raina wiped her knives clean on the curtains.

"Who were they?" Nola asked.

"Two outsiders who picked a really bad time to raid this house," Raina said. "You hear that up there? If we hadn't paid you a visit, you'd all be dead."

"I can't believe it's gotten this bad so quickly," Nola said. "Breaking into people's houses?"

"If they have candles, what else might they have?" Kieran stepped through the window, a bow in hand and a quiver of arrows over his shoulder. He grabbed the bloody arrow from the floor and pulled the other from the wall, adding both to his supply.

"But then they're just killing each other," Nola said. "There won't be anyone left."

"Exactly," Raina said. "Soon, only the strong and the sneaky will be alive. Welcome to the end of the world."

"We should go." Julian pushed away from the wall, giving his shoulders a tentative shake.

Raina stepped out through the window.

"We need to find Gentry," Jeremy said. "She'll know what's happening."

"We'll just walk right on up to the domes and knock on the door," Raina said. "Ask if we can talk to your sister."

Nola stepped out into the night. The cold tickled her back. She reached behind. Her shirt had been sliced open, and blood slicked her fingers.

"Damn." She reached back through the window, wiping her fingers on the curtains.

"Kieran, keep an arm around Julian," Raina said. "If he starts to fall behind, carry him."

"Nola." Kieran held out the bow and quiver. "Can you take these?"

"I don't know how to use them." Nola let Kieran pass her the hand-carved weapons.

"I just need you to carry them." Kieran winked.

"I can do that part." Nola looped the quiver over one shoulder and the bow over the other.

"Lover boy with me." Raina walked out through the grass, ignoring the two bodies crumpled on the lawn. "And keep your gun out. We might have made a bit of noise."

But you won. They'll leave us alone because you won.

Nola swallowed the childish sentiment as they reached the cracked road. The time for speaking seemed to have ended, though no one gave the order.

She examined every shadow as they moved down the street. Every rustling leaf was a killer aiming an arrow at her heart. Every house held a dozen people waiting to attack.

They moved more slowly, keeping to a human running pace.

A wide circle of ashes and debris covered the center of the road. Three unburnt bodies lay nearby. The animals had already begun their work on the corpses. Nola shuddered and focused on staring at the back of Jeremy's head. Blood stained his hair, and tiny flecks of glass sparkled in the strands.

Raina didn't slow her pace until they reached the edge of the highway.

Tents and huts had been built in a clump in the center of the wide road. Soot stains covered the fabric of the tents. Nola's eyes watered at the stench of human filth wafting from the ramshackle village.

"Stupid." Raina shook her head. "Do they think the Domers are going to help them? Do they think the city being gone is going to get rid of the acid in the clouds before the spring rains?"

"Let them believe what they like," Julian said. "The illusion of safety is the best they can hope for."

"We could raid it," Raina said. "Force them into safer dwellings."

"No time." Kieran pointed east.

Gray tinted the sky.

"We've got the suits," Raina said.

"We should get to ground," Jeremy said. "Julian's suit already has a hole in it, and he's still recovering."

"Where do we go?" Nola looked toward the city. There wasn't a single building in sight that hadn't been ruined by the fire. There would be no way to know which buildings were stable.

"If we're going to play in the city, we're going home." Raina threw one last glare at the tents and strode across the highway.

"Might it not be better to go somewhere a touch more discreet?" Julian asked.

"The tunnels of Nightland were made for us," Raina said. "We're going to ground there."

"The Outer Guard know where the entrance is," Jeremy said. "If I were stuck patrolling a burned out city, that's where I'd shelter."

"Weren't you just asking for a family reunion?" Raina said.

"They'll have the advantage if they've barricaded themselves in there," Jeremy said. "We don't know how many of them there are, what sorts of weapons they have—"

"So what's your plan, lover boy?" Raina asked. "Wait around for the end of the world to come? Head on over to the tunnels and sit on the sidewalk, waiting for someone to come out with a roll call and supply list?"

"I go check and see if the tunnels are clear," Nola said.

"No," Kieran said at the same time Jeremy said, "Absolutely not."

"I know the tunnels well enough to be able to find out if anyone's down there and get back out," Nola said. "I can be quick."

"I'll go in," Jeremy said. "If the Outer Guard are down there—"

"Then you're a deserter," Nola said.

"And they put out a kill order on you," Jeremy said.

"I've got a great idea," Raina said. "You both go in, poke around, and see what there is to see. Then if you're not dead, you come back up and give us a wave."

"Who's to say they won't kill them on sight?" Kieran said. "It's too dangerous."

"We're going into the tunnels, and someone has to go first," Raina said. "They won't hesitate to go for the heart of a vampire, but maybe Gentry and her little guard friends will be a bit slower to kill her brother and his girlfriend."

"We could go some—"

"Jeremy and I will go." Nola interrupted Kieran. "We'll go see who's down there and come right back out."

Raina turned off of Main, following a narrow alley between blackened ruins. "Perfect. We'll find a place to watch the exit. Nola and Jeremy, go in and scout."

Kieran shook his head but didn't argue as he and Julian followed Raina.

"Nola." Jeremy walked right behind her shoulder. "I can go in on my own, or take Kieran with me. He knows the tunnels better than you do."

"I want to stay with you," Nola said. "You jumped through that window and I didn't know where you were going or if someone had hurt you. I hated that feeling, and I don't want to do it again. You don't just get to worry about me, Jeremy. I get to worry about you, too."

"I love you," Jeremy said.

"Good," Nola said. "Because you're stuck with me."

"That's what I'm hoping for."

Nola could hear the smile in his voice, but the burned out buildings stole the joy from her heart. Melted metal twisted up from the charred remains of the city. Piles of brick and stone littered the street.

The scent of smoke, burned rubber, and decay sent sour rolling into Nola's mouth. She pulled her shirt up over her nose, but the stench penetrated the thin fabric.

There were no street signs left or any landmarks Nola could recognize, but Raina steered them through the city without hesitation.

A *clatter* and *crash* sounded in a nearby building. Nola wrenched her knives from their sheathes, her heart racing. Before the blades were fully free, a cat ran across the street.

Most of the poor creature's fur had been burned away. The cat hissed as it ran across their path and dodged out of sight.

Run before someone eats you.

The ground crunched beneath their feet as they moved deeper into the city. Nola didn't look down to find out why. She was too afraid of what the answer might be.

She looked up to the lightening sky instead. Orange tinted the horizon.

Hurry, Raina.

As if Raina had heard her thoughts, she waved the group toward a tilted building. The roof had burned entirely away, leaving only a shaft of brick behind.

Raina held up a hand, stopping the others as she stalked silently up the steps.

The quiet of the dawn pounded in Nola's ears. She reached for Jeremy. His hand found hers. A minute passed. Then two.

Finally, Raina stepped back out onto the stoop. She pointed to Julian and Kieran, waving them into the house, then to Nola and Jeremy, pointing the two of them across the street.

Kieran turned to Nola, a line creasing his brow. She could hear his voice in her mind. *Don't go. It won't be safe.*

I know you too well, Kieran.

Nola shook her head and passed the bow and quiver to Kieran. Her hand lingered on his for a moment.

He looked to Jeremy and gave him a nod, then turned and disappeared into the shadows of the bricks, Julian right behind him.

Pain scratched at Nola's chest.

Call after him. Tell him to be careful.

But silence filled the city, muting her voice.

Words don't belong on the streets anymore.

Jeremy laid a hand on her shoulder. She turned away from the leaning bricks, following the warmth of his touch across the street.

The building in front of them had collapsed entirely. Not even the stone steps stayed standing. A giant hole in the ground had eaten the stoop.

Twisted and torn metal stairs reached into the hole and out of sight.

Jeremy held up three fingers then pointed into the ground with his gun.

He lowered one finger at a time, counting down.

One.

Nola's heart quickened as she watched his first finger fold. This is where it had all begun, at the door to Nightland.

Two.

The sun found its way over the horizon, giving depth to the shadows of the devastated city. The world had crumbled so quickly. Soon there would be nothing left but stone and ash.

Three.

Together, they jumped into the ruins of Nightland.

Nola's journey concludes in Son of Sun. *Order your copy today.*

NOLA'S JOURNEY CONCLUDES IN...

ESCAPE INTO ADVENTURE

Thank you for reading *Night of Never*. If you enjoyed the book, please consider leaving a review to help other readers discover the series.

As always, thanks for reading,

Megan O'Russell

Never miss a moment of the danger or romance.

Join the Megan O'Russell mailing list to stay up to date on all the action by visiting https://www.meganorussell.com/book-signup.

ABOUT THE AUTHOR

 Megan O'Russell is the author of several Young Adult series that invite readers to escape into worlds of adventure. From *Girl of Glass*, which blends dystopian darkness with the heart-pounding danger of vampires, to *Ena of Ilbrea*, which draws readers into an epic world of magic and assassins.

With the *Girl of Glass* series, *The Tethering* series, *The Chronicles of Maggie Trent*, *The Tale of Bryant Adams,* the *Ena of Ilbrea* series, and several more projects planned, there are always exciting new books on the horizon. To be the first to hear about new releases, free short stories, and giveaways, sign up for Megan's newsletter by visiting the following:

https://www.meganorussell.com/book-signup.

Originally from Upstate New York, Megan is a professional musical theatre performer whose work has taken her across North America. Her chronic wanderlust has led her from Alaska to Thailand and many places in between. Wanting to travel has fostered Megan's love of books that allow her to visit countless new worlds from her favorite reading nook. Megan is also a lyricist and playwright. Information on her theatrical works can be found at RussellCompositions.com.

She would be thrilled to chat with you on Facebook or Twitter

@MeganORussell, elated if you'd visit her website MeganORussell.com, and over the moon if you'd like the pictures of her adventures on Instagram @ORussellMegan.

ALSO BY MEGAN O'RUSSELL

Mountain and Ash

Ice and Sky

Feather and Flame

<u>Guilds of Ilbrea</u>

Inker and Crown

Myth and Storm

<u>Heart of Smoke</u>

Heart of Smoke

Soul of Glass

Eye of Stone

Ash of Ages